# Crossfire

## A P Bateman

Crossfire

Copyright © 2026 by A P Bateman

All rights reserved.

No part of this book may be reproduced in any form or by any electronic or mechanical means, including information storage and retrieval systems, without written permission from the author, except for the use of brief quotations in a book review.

*For Clair, Summer and Lewis*

# Also by A P Bateman

**The Alex King Series**

The Contract Man

Lies and Retribution

Shadows of Good Friday

The Five

Reaper

Stormbound

Breakout

From the Shadows

Rogue

The Asset

Last Man Standing

Hunter Killer

The Congo Contract

Dead Man Walking

Sovereign Power

Kingmaker

Untouchable

The Enemy

Die Trying

All the King's Men

The Eagle's Talon

Backlash

Old Scores

Crossfire

**The Rob Stone Series**

The Ares Virus

The Town

The Island

Stone Cold

The Cartel

1600

**The DCI Grant Series**

Vice

Taken

**Standalone Novels**

The Most Dangerous Game

Never Go Back

**Novellas**

The Perfect Murder?

Atonement

# Chapter One
## Uganda-Tanzania Border, Twenty Years Ago

The right arm of the free-world. It should have been a pen or a chequebook. Perhaps even a bible. But it was a FN FAL rifle, and it was in King's hands, but he felt anything but free. Its barrel was scalding hot, the stock sticky from the blood of its last owner, and it was all that stood between him and the thirty Ugandan government forces intent on killing him.

There was movement in the jungle behind him, and King picked up a spare magazine for the rifle before dragging one of the bodies by its ankle and dropping it in front of another body, before laying down behind his makeshift barrier.

King reached for another magazine on the corpse in front of him, tugging it out from the man's otherwise depleted bandolier. He wasn't certain if the bodies would afford him protection from enemy bullets, but they did at least shield him from view and provide the rifle with a steady rest. He needed to make every shot count, and it was imperative that he dropped the first soldiers who stepped out from cover because watching your comrades fall quickly usually got a man's attention. Behind him, if Stewart was still alive, and still carried Moffusa Bentuwi on his back like a sack of maize through the jungle, then he was their ticket out of here. No Bentuwi, no ride home. The pilot would wait for the country's legitimate choice for presidential successor, but he would be wheels up at first sight of two white mercenaries staggering out of the jungle alone, let alone with half the Ugandan army in pursuit. The pilot had already been paid half his fee to get Bentuwi out and he would not get the other half of his fee without him, and he wouldn't give a damn about just King and Stewart, who would be more trouble than it was worth.

The first man through the brush was barely a man. King did not want to think about his age, because an AK47 was as dangerous in a boy's hands as in anybody else's. His eyes were keen, but that keenness was derived only through fear. He stepped over the body of one of his comrades, his eyes everywhere at once. Another soldier stepped into the clearing, older, wiser. He had allowed the boy to go first. There was no love lost in battle.

King checked his watch, mentally doing the maths. It was three miles to the extraction point, and he had thirty-two minutes to do it. Stewart might manage to convince the pilot to wait at the business end of a gun, but even then, the tough Scotsman would have his own deadline and if King did not meet it then it would be wheels up and out of there, and he knew that the bastard wouldn't lose a wink of sleep over it. Not now the mission had gone tits up, and they had lost control of a member of their team. Peter Stewart would be thinking of little more than damage limitation and cutting loose ends.

A third Soldier entered the clearing, and then a fourth. That ought to be about right. More than that and if he had a

**Crossfire**

weapon malfunction or took a bullet, then he would not be able to control the situation. He had seen firsthand what the Ugandan forces did to prisoners, and he had been left under no illusion that it would mean curtains if that happened.

King shot the boy between the eyes, then fired three shots centre mass at the second man. Two more double taps and the other two went down. He backed up into the brush as all hell broke out, and muzzle flashes lit the dull undergrowth like a hundred fireflies. He swapped to a new magazine, tucking the used one with twelve remaining rounds into his pocket for later. With a 7.62x51mm round already chambered, he had twenty-one shots remaining. Having taken just a few steps into the brush, he pulled the pin on a frag and tossed the grenade behind him into the clearing. There was no flame, no men catapulting into the air, but three of the enemy went down, fragmentation shrapnel cutting their legs, bodies and faces to pieces. The rest of the soldiers gave the clearing a wide berth, and as they skirted the treeline they wasted precious minutes while King sprinted full-pace through the undergrowth. Pulling the pin on a smoke grenade, he tossed it behind him and kept running. Behind him, orange smoke billowed in the wind, slowing his pursuers as they decided against running blindly into the dense, orange fog. King stopped and turned around, bracing the weapon against the trunk of a tree as he fired groups of three shots in a progressive arc until the weapon clicked empty. He reloaded, then tossed a fragmentation grenade high in the air and counted off five seconds, which was about the time it took to complete its arc and detonate the moment it hit the ground. He heard the solid thud, followed by screams, and he tossed the last of his smoke grenades into the trees, turned and sprinted through the undergrowth having significantly slowed their progress.

King checked his watch again. It was going to be close. Stewart was way ahead of him now, and he had the man that they had set out to free. Why would Stewart wait for him? He had what he came for, and because of one team member, civil war had broken out and genocide in neighbouring Rwanda was now a harsh, ugly reality. Questions would be asked, and Stewart wouldn't want any contradictions in his story. MI6 would batten down the hatches so anybody not singing from the same hymn sheet would be a problem. If Stewart took off with Moffusa Bentuwi, and King met his fate at the hands of the Ugandan army, then there would be nobody around to refute Stewart's 'truth'. Now that the thought had come to him, King could think of little else. There was no guarantee that even if he reached the extraction point in time, Stewart would hold the helicopter. Stewart could order the pilot to take off the moment he got there. Moffusa Bentuwi was the objective. Stewart wouldn't risk failure waiting for a junior operative with just three years' experience in the field. That wasn't something the Scotsman would risk his pension on. It wasn't even something the man would risk his next drink on. Stewart had lost Richard Collins, to lose King would set him back, but there were mouldable young men in the army, perhaps even in prison, that Stewart could train and shape for future missions. He'd done it before, and he'd do it again.

King checked his watch again. It would be tight, but he could do it. The distance with the time remaining would be challenging if he was wearing trainers and running kit, and as part of a nice, flat park run. In torn and soaked fatigues and wearing heavy boots and carrying twenty pounds of kit and ammunition and a ten-pound loaded rifle, it was another matter entirely. The terrain was undulating, thick with brush and scattered with rocks, and strewn with sun-bleached carcasses that had sustained both land and fauna for millennia. He could do it. He knew he could. But what if he could not shake off the soldiers behind him? What if Stewart did not wait to the extraction zero hour? He would arrive in a state of exhaustion – he had already been on the go for forty-eight hours without rest – he would not be able to keep fighting and would surely be captured – and that would mean that he would become a political bargaining chip. MI6 would deny his very existence – as well they could, because of Stewart's secretive department with no links to the Secret Intelligence Service – and President Yoweri K. Museveni would not only be out for blood, but would parade King in front of the world's media to strengthen his support from the African Union, whose member states had been most critical of his tyrannical regime.

King stopped in his tracks, turned and knelt beside a large baobab tree, its thick trunk capable of stopping any bullet short of an anti-aircraft round. He pressed his stomach and chest into the soft bark, grateful for its protection, brought the weapon up to aim. He would have preferred it if the weapon had been fitted with a decent optic, but beggars couldn't be choosers. He had just killed a man for it, and up until then, he had engaged the enemy with just his 9mm Browning pistol after abandoning his rifle when he had run out of ammunition. King removed the bandolier that he had also relieved one of the dead men of and dropped it on the ground beside him. The bergen followed. All that he carried on his person now was a two-pint water bottle, his holstered pistol and sheath knife.

King steadied himself, eyes fixed on the dense undergrowth. He caught a flicker of movement among the trees and held his breath, waiting for confirmation. After a moment, three men materialised from the brush, their approach marked by an unnatural stillness. They moved cautiously, reminiscent of deer picking their way through the mist at dawn, alert to every sound and shadow. The tension in the air was palpable as King braced for what would come next, knowing that every decision in this moment could mean the difference between survival and death. He placed the iron sights on the first man, a post on the fore-end and a ringed aperture, or ghost ring, at the rear. He was aiming for centre mass. The spinal column was the goal, but if his aim was off that left the heart, aorta, and lungs. His finger tightened on the trigger, and taking a deep breath, he squeezed. The rifle leapt in his hands, the stock hammering into his shoulder, but he was already moving the sights to the second man and he fired again, and then at the third. All three men went down. Two of them resting still, the third man writhing on the ground and screaming. King left the man alone. Not because he was feeling particularly merciful, but because the man may have friends who would attend to him, and in doing so, put more strain on the enemy force. He had one last fragmentation grenade remaining, and he wedged it underneath his discarded bergen and pulled the pin. There was little point exhausting himself to make the extraction; he wasn't even sure that Stewart would wait, anyway. He needed a Plan B. Something that would give him options if he did not make the extraction point in time, something he could switch to if he ended up a mile short and was too exhausted to fight. Backing away from the wounded soldier and the sounds of men pressing onwards through the brush, King checked the compass hanging around his neck underneath his tattered shirt, soaked in both blood and sweat. Almost all of Uganda was to the north and he had burned his bridges there. The

**Crossfire**

LRA thugs were to the west, and killing everyone who stood in their way, and Rwanda had broken into civil war to the south. Which left Tanzania to the east. Jakaya Kikwete had just won a landslide election with eighty per cent of the vote, and the country was in jubilant spirits. The army was pressing west to secure the border with Rwanda succumbing to genocide, and if the Tutsis were overrun, then a mass migration crisis would see the border flooded with war refugees. If he could get through, he had a contact in the press who was covering the election victory, and something to do with orphanages losing government funding. King did not have friends, but he considered his press contact, a former lover, would be as close to a friend as he had. It was certainly worth a try.

## Chapter Two
### Two Weeks Earlier, Whitehall, London

"Take a seat, King," said Stewart gruffly. He pointed to the chair next to Richard Collins, but King walked around the table and sat opposite him, both men either side of Stewart who was seated at the head of the table. "Glad that you're finally here..." the tough Scotsman added.

King shrugged. "You said, zero-nine-hundred, and it's zero-nine-hundred."

"Work to rule, eh?" Collins said sardonically.

King ignored him. Timing was everything. Collins had been ten minutes late for the extraction on their last job in Beirut and it had cost the informant his life. The job had been such a shit show that King had seen no stock in telling Stewart about his latest recruit's shortcomings, but he would have thought that Collins would know when to jibe and when to shut the fuck up.

"You two work well together, so here we are again with job number five," said Stewart.

"Fifth time's a charm..." Collins muttered under his breath.

In front of Stewart were two files, and he slid one across the table to each of them. "Moffusa Bentuwi," he said, allowing the two men to study the photograph in front of them. He was nothing remarkable. Thin, greying hair but with a kind face. His skin was as black as coal, which made the whites of his eyes look brighter, and they bore through the photograph with an intensity of both passion and intelligence. "The true President of Uganda, if anecdotal evidence is to be believed, which means that Jakaya Kikwete's landslide victory wasn't all that it seemed."

King didn't look up as he read. This would be his third African job, and the other two still gave him nightmares. But what's more, he didn't trust Collins and was no happier working with him again. There had been the hit on the Russian spy in Paris, the bank job to get into a member of the House of Lord's safety deposit box – who had a lucrative side hustle selling secrets – the Serbian war criminal who they had snatched in Madrid, and finally; the shit show that had been Beirut. Three of those operations had gone well, but Beirut would have far-reaching consequences, not only for MI6 and Mossad, but for the entire region. King knew that he had not heard the last of it.

"And you want Jakaya Kikwete dead and Moffusa Bentuwi installed in his place," King ventured.

"Easier said than done, but yes, along those lines," Stewart replied. "Anyway, we don't want him dead. We want him deposed. The last thing Central Africa needs is another bloody martyr."

"Swapping one kaffir for another," Collins commented flatly. "For all the difference it will make..."

"I don't like that term," said King

.Collins shrugged. "You haven't had to live with them,

bru." He paused. "In Zimbabwe they tried to steal our land..."

"A white man complaining about stolen African land," King rolled his eyes.

"You know nothing, bru... the trouble with Africa is that for every Mandela or Desmond Tutu, there's a kaffir who is not long down from the trees. They're no different here, just look at your crime statistics..."

"My brother is mixed race," King said coldly before he could stop himself. His namesake, the basis of his new identity was an only child. King may have had siblings in his former life, but no more. That life had belonged to Mark Jeffries, and Mark Jeffries was a murderer who drowned in a bog escaping Dartmoor Prison. There was no going back, and never to be a mention of his past. Stewart had been most insistent upon that. He glanced at Stewart, but the man looked away in annoyance.

"Your mother wasn't fussy, then?" Collins smirked.

King ignored the jibe. Self-control was something that he had been working on, but that didn't stop him wanting to stick his knife in the man's neck all the same. He couldn't see what Stewart saw in the man. Collins enjoyed killing and had manipulated situations to satiate his appetite for death. King had killed in the service of his country, but he did not enjoy it. He was comfortable doing it but had never found pleasure in it. Killing was something that occasionally had to be done. It also irked him that he had not mentioned that Collins' timekeeping had cost them their asset's life. There was no stock in telling Stewart now, but he had already made up his mind that he would not cover for the man again.

"I feel like I may have to bash your heads together like a

couple of squabbling brothers," said Stewart. "But here's the deal. Get the fuck along, or one of you is out..."

King glanced at Collins, who was staring back at him with a sly grin on his face, but he could not maintain his stare. His glacier blue eyes bored into his own and Collins looked away, visibly uncomfortable. He distracted himself with the file, then after a moment said, "If we kill Jakaya Kikwete, what's to say his army will support Moffusa Bentuwi?" Collins paused. "They may just execute him and find another puppet dictator."

"He just said he didn't want Kikwete dead, so it's not a fucking option. And why don't you finish reading the report before saying something dumb?" King asked impatiently. "The report concludes that Moffusa Bentuwi was the likely popular vote, and that there is only one known military leader with any sway over congress. Jakaya Kikwete had enough support in congress because of his association with General Mantutsi. Remove this Mantutsi bloke and Kikwete loses his military ally."

"I hadn't got to that part yet," Collins protested.

"Then don't ask stupid questions," King replied. "Or up your reading speed by changing up your genre. I mean, re-reading *Spot Has a Red Ball* or *The Tiger Who Came to Tea*, isn't going to improve things for you..."

"Didn't you just hear me?" Stewart growled.

"Sorry, boss," Collins replied.

King said nothing. The asset's blood was on the man's hands in Beirut, and King had been tempted to shoot Collins in the back of his head when they switched cars outside the city. He only wished he had because he was about to go into Central Africa and expect the man to have his back.

"I'll recruit some help. Collins, you're on equipment and local assets," said Stewart, ignoring King's refusal to apologise. "King, you're going to do a recce. It's right up your street. Nobody to fall out with, and nobody to answer to. You go in, don't get yourself caught, and return with photographs, details of troop movements and the whereabouts of Moffusa Bentuwi and General Mantutsi. Oh, and the LRA, the Lord's Resistance Army, is a rabble who enjoy lopping the limbs off anyone who disagrees with their beliefs, and they are operating in the area, and along the borders of Congo and Rwanda."

King nodded. Just like that. Another impossible situation to navigate, that was apparently in his country's interest. His only problem now, was where to start.

## Chapter Three
### Entebbe International Airport, Uganda

King slipped his arm around the woman's waist, prompting her to smile warmly as she glanced up at him. She responded to his gesture with a gentle kiss on his cheek, their affection clear even under the watchful gaze of the border control officer in front of them. The officer, having just stamped the passport of the man ahead of them in the line, fixed them with a stern look, perhaps unimpressed by their public display of affection. Undeterred, King stepped forwards, leading the way, and presented both his and the woman's passports to the official for inspection.

"One at a time. Step back behind the yellow line," the official told them with a sneer of disdain.

King apologised and took back his own passport while Ginnie Blake stood in front of the desk and King toed the line.

"Nature of your travel?"

"Holiday," Ginnie replied warmly.

"Just holiday?"

"Yes."

"No business?"

"No," she smiled.

The official flicked through her passport, pausing over the visa stamps. "You like to travel?" he asked. "You have been to a great many countries."

"It's my thing..." she replied, then added, "*Our* thing..."

King found himself involuntarily holding his breath, then exhaled deeply, relieved when the official stamped Ginnie's passport with more than ten-times the effort required.

"Next!"

King found himself grinning somewhat inanely as he handed the man his own passport for the second time. The border official was perched awkwardly on a swivel bar stool, his considerable bulk causing him to spill over the sides. His stomach protruded over trousers that were far too tight, emphasising his dishevelled appearance. Dark stains marked the fabric beneath both his armpits; evidence of long hours spent in the stuffy confines of the border post. From the other side of the desk, King could catch a whiff of the man's sour body odour, pungent enough to make him nearly gag. A holster hung loosely from the official's belt, drawing King's attention. The revolver it contained showed signs of heavy use: the blueing was all but worn away, and the frame was speckled with rust, suggesting it had not been properly maintained for some time.

"Your wife likes to travel."

"Girlfriend," he corrected him. "Yes, she does. We both do. That's how we met."

"How long are you intending to stay in Uganda?"

King hadn't heard the man ask Ginnie, but that didn't mean that he hadn't. The air was filled with the usual bustle of airports in the Third World. He knew that the phrase wasn't meant to be used since the end of the Cold War, but he still thought of certain countries that way. Developing World, or Least Developed World would sum up Uganda, like many African nations. "Two weeks," he replied, sticking to the cover story. "But we may travel overland to Kenya. We are still very much undecided."

"Has Uganda not got enough to entertain you?" the man stared at him. "It is a beautiful country, with many wonderful things to experience."

"No, I'm sure it has. That's why we're here, after all." The official stared at King, and normally able to stare anyone down, King averted his eyes because he knew that this was all about power and he had to be the grey man in this situation. His passport was stamped with as much effort as the people in the queue before him, and King was surprised that the desk was still standing.

"Well, at least we're in," said King as he caught up with Ginnie.

She smiled back at him. Tanned, freckled, and with her brunette hair tied back in a loose ponytail, the ends of her hair golden blonde, or balayage. She looked every bit the traveller, and every bit the next woman that King wanted in his bed. "Taxi, hotel, beer and a swim," she said. "And in that order."

"Then dinner and bed," King added. "Separate beds, of course."

"It'll be a double bed, as per the cover," she replied. "We'll just have to top and tail…"

"Can't say that sounds altogether terrible," he grinned. "Sometimes it's preferable…"

She punched him playfully on the arm. "Stop it," she said, then added, "I might like it…" They had built a good rapport on the two six-hour flights to get here, but King could not yet tell if her friendly banter and flirting indicated that she would be happy with more.

Outside in the mid-afternoon humidity they declined a dozen taxi drivers and headed for one parked on its own further down the thoroughfare. The driver got out and donned a blue and white New York Yankees baseball cap, which clashed somewhat with his red Manchester United football strip, but it at least made him easy to identify. Stewart had set up the meet, having used the driver before. He had proved himself trustworthy and was making a few months' salary from a few days at King's disposal.

"Taxi, *muzungu*?" the man asked, using the slang for a white man from the Bantu language. "Good price..."

King nodded and handed the man his leather holdall, while Ginnie smiled and positioned her small pull-along near the trunk of the white Toyota Corolla. The taxi driver lifted both bags into the boot and slammed the lid down as they both got into the rear. "The Emin Pasha Hotel, Kampala," said King. "Do you know it?"

"Sure do, *muzungu*, it brand new. It like a small palace!" He started the engine and pulled out into traffic leaving the airport. After just three hundred metres the traffic was not merely cars and taxis, but overloaded wagons, buses packed with twice as many passengers that they had been designed or rated for, and heavily laden donkeys. Oxen pulled carts and bicycles were everywhere. "I am David," the driver told them.

King already knew, but he nodded in the man's rearview mirror but did not tell the man his name.

Ginnie glanced at King and smiled. "This is kind of an assault on the senses," she said, looking back out of the window. "I usually go to the Greek Islands or Majorca each summer. This is wild. Look, there's a woman and four kids on that moped!" She paused. "*And* two bags of groceries!"

King smiled. Ginnie's passport, along with the visa stamps, was a document of pure fiction. He wasn't even sure if Ginnie was her actual name. She had been chosen by Peter Stewart to be arm candy, nothing more. She would, in fact, remain at the hotel after King left in the morning, where she would order food and drinks and enjoy the pool and gardens for a few days, then fly out of Entebbe and back to her job in MI6 as an office manager in administration and payroll. Stewart had reasoned that secretaries were generally eager to help in an operation, forever knowing that they played a small part in the world of espionage outside of the office and the claustrophobic walls of the River House. They would go to their beds with their husbands two decades from now, with a secret they could never tell, and never certain how important the part they had played but always imagining that they had helped save the world. In some cases, they had.

King paid David the taxi fare, despite him already being paid handsomely by Peter Stewart, because that kept the man's cover clean and appearances were everything. Despite earning good money out of his deal with Peter Stewart, Uganda was an impoverished country, and King was only too pleased to part with a few dollars. King liked to use American dollars when he could in Asia and Africa as it was readily accepted and added a veil of anonymity to his activities. They were met by a porter who, despite King's protests, took his holdall from him and pulled Ginnie's wheeled pull along up the paved pathway to the colonial style buildings. Palms lined the paths, and the lawns either side of the paths were neatly trimmed and perfectly edged. Water features including shallow, square koi carp ponds joined by narrow moats, and fountains added an air of serenity, the bustle and chaos of the streets outside feeling a world away. King tipped the porter, and he must have got it right because he beamed a brilliant white smile and thanked them both as he headed back outside. King checked them in with the female receptionist, who summoned another porter – this time dressed a little more formally in tan trousers and a crisp, white shirt and black tie. The man was friendly, but people in the tip business generally were, and he showed them around the suite, including the balcony which looked down over a small kidney shaped pool and quiet sun terrace. Once again, King parted with ten dollars because he didn't have a five, and when the door was closed, he kicked off his shoes and threw himself onto the bed.

"This will do," said Ginnie. "A few days beside the pool drinking mojitos and reading some trashy paperbacks, I don't think I could be happier!"

"And make sure you rack up a decent sized bill with room service," said King. "The *company* can afford it."

"Room service?" she said looking disappointed.

King shrugged. "We don't want it to look too obvious that I'm no longer here. Perhaps you should sun yourself and read on the balcony and keep the personal appearances down to the odd dip in the pool..."

"Now, it's beginning to sound more like work..." she replied despondently, before kicking off her shoes. She then peeled off her jeans and tugged off her vest top, standing before him in her bra and pants, "I'm going to take a shower," she said. "You must need one, too..."

King nodded and watched her as she headed into the bathroom. She had a terrific figure, and he could tell that she worked out, given that he could see so much of her, wearing so little. He heard the shower running and imagined what she would look like naked. He looked out of the window, brilliant white clouds scudding across the deep blue sky. There was a depth of blue over the skies of Africa that never seemed to be replicated in Europe. Big skies. Skies you otherwise only ever saw far out at sea. King lost himself in the heavens as he listened to the running water, then it dawned on him. She was taking a shower and had commented that he must need one, too. *You bloody idiot, Mark,* he thought. He had dropped the name in all but thought and had yet to refer to himself within his internal monologue as 'Alex'. King got off the bed and stripped to his boxer shorts. There was still a chance that he had misunderstood her intentions, so he hid his dignity as well as her chances for embarrassment. She hadn't locked the door, which was a good sign, and as he stepped inside the bathroom, steam filling the air and the mirrors thick and opaque with condensation, she looked at him, foamy soap covering her breasts and little else. Water ran off her glistening body in rivulets, and she smiled as he walked closer.

"I was wondering if you were ever going to get the hint," she chided.

King pulled off his boxers and stepped inside, the spray hitting his chest and filling the wet-room with fine mist. "Sorry, I was a bit slow," he replied, taking her in his arms.

"Slow?" Ginnie smiled. "Trust me, that's something I really don't want you to be. Not in here, at least. Sex in the shower consists mainly of taking turns to avoid drowning, or being cold…"

## Chapter Four
### Mwanza, Tanzania

"These are junk," said Collins, dropping the AK74 back into the crate.

"They are a good weapon, very reliable..." the man paused, unable to hide his annoyance. "They are better than the AK47, a big improvement."

"Yeah, when they were made, perhaps, but these haven't been stripped and cleaned properly in ten years. Show me what else you have or I'll take my money elsewhere."

Fusa tried and failed not to let the anger show and was angered further when he saw how the Afrikaans seemed to enjoy toying with him. He picked up the crowbar and prised open another crate. Standing at six foot six, he had no idea how heavy he was but was at least twice the weight of the average man he came up against, and he was used to his size being an imposing quality. He never had to ask somebody to do something twice, and he never got asked to do something that he did not want to do. The fact that the Afrikaans man did not seem to care, had actually goaded him as he had shown him his stock, both confused and worried him. "FN FAL, British versions, known as the SLR." he said, pulling a rifle from the crate packed with straw.

"Too heavy and cumbersome," Collins replied without looking. Fusa shook his head and replaced the rifle before wiping the thick oil off his hands on the seat of his worn and faded jeans. "What about M16s?"

Fusa wiped his brow with his muscled forearm, but it did not seem to make much difference. The barn was hot and airless, with chickens packed into nesting boxes at the far end and a broken-down Massey Ferguson tractor from the nineteen-sixties propped up on bricks, its wheels removed and in a state of half-forgotten repair. "Are you fighting Hutus or Tutsis?"

"I can't say."

The big man shrugged. "Gangs take much khat, many drugs. You want seven-point-six-two, not tiny five-point-five-six. One shot good, five shots, bad..." He jemmied open another crate, tossed the crowbar onto the dusty earth and lifted out a Heckler & Koch G3 rifle.

Collins nodded approvingly. The rifles would have been a little shorter than the FN FAL, but these were fitted with folding stocks so were considerably shorter and lighter. He could see that there were thirty-round magazines in the box instead of the standard twenty. He took the rifle from Fusa and checked it over, before working the action and examining the breech and barrel. It was an accurate and reliable weapon, and he would have to agree with the arms dealer that 7.62x51mm packed a hell of a punch and had a considerable range advantage over modern NATO assault rifles. The rifles were well oiled and although far from new, as good as he was going to get in Central Africa with wars and conflict in every other surrounding country over the past ten years.

"How many in the crate?"

"Four."

"I'll take them," said Collins. "And four of the FALs. Six magazines for each..." He looked at the green metal ammunition boxes with two hundred and fifty rounds of 7.62x51mm stamped in skewwhiff yellow writing. "And four of those."

Fusa's demeanour shifted instantly; the irritation he had previously shown towards the Afrikaans man vanished in a heartbeat. A wide grin spread across his face, replacing his earlier scowl. Clearly pleased with the turn of events and the successful sale, he clapped his large hands together in satisfaction. Without hesitation, he turned towards the young boy who had been waiting quietly by the door throughout the negotiations. With a sharp command, Fusa instructed the boy to begin packing up the requested firearms, magazines, and ammunition for their customer, ensuring that the transaction would be completed efficiently and without further delay.

"Pistols," Collins said.

"Browning nine millimetre?"

"Fine. Eight of them, with sixteen magazines, and enough ammunition to fill them." He paused. "And something small. A back-up piece."

"Makarov?" Fusa offered. "I can sell you eight of those as well."

"I just need one," Collins replied. "With two magazines." Fusa nodded. Collins could see that the man was disappointed not to get seven more guns into the sale, but he had done well already. The Makarov was solely insurance for Collins, he wouldn't tell anybody about it, least of all

King or Stewart. He didn't trust anybody in this life and was still alive only because of his distrust.

"Grenades?"

"Frags?"

"And smoke."

"A dozen of each should do it."

"You are starting a small war?" Fusa grinned.

"You ask too many questions, Kaffir..."

Fusa glared at Collins, his anger at the racial slur evident in his eyes. However, the practical side of his character soon prevailed. Business was business. He suppressed his irritation, turning away to assist the boy in packing the requested weapons and ammunition into two separate crates. The transaction, although tense, was ultimately driven by the business at hand rather than personal feelings. He took the Makarov and two magazines and handed them to Collins, along with a handful of 9x18mm Makarov ammunition. The deal was almost done. Some people were more difficult than others, and the wiry Afrikaans was one of those clients.

Collins loaded both magazines and put the few remaining rounds into his left pocket along with the spare magazine. He loaded the weapon and made it ready before slipping it into his right pocket. Fusa and the boy took the crates out to his Toyota Landcruiser then returned for the crate of ammunition and the grenades. Collins took the small backpack off his shoulders and checked the money. Stewart had provided him with a contact, who had in turn recommended Fusa. He had provided him with the operating capital, too. Collins had fifteen thousand US dollars to play with for the weaponry, and receipts were certainly not required. Men like Fusa didn't do receipts, and people like Stewart didn't ask for them.

Collins ambled over to the weathered doors, the planks twisted and warped from the harsh African sun. Outside, Fusa had parked next to the hired Toyota, his battered blue pickup the ideal vehicle for transporting heavy equipment while remaining under the radar. The man had supplied most of the warlords in a dozen African nations, and still he looked like a simple farmer. Collins shielded his eyes against the glare of the sun and looked out over the landscape, which was a mixture of farmland, scrubland and pockets of surviving jungle. A distant farmhouse was Fusa's nearest neighbour. The man had the perfect cover with the watermelon farm, that aside from watering and performing sweeps for pests every few days, relied on casual labour three times a year for harvesting and packing.

His phone's text alert vibrated in his pocket, and he took out his phone and read the text message. It was unexpected, but not unwelcome, and he read it a second time trying to digest it and calculate the possibility. With a shrug, Collins put his phone away and wandered back inside as Fusa and the young boy returned. The boy started packing away the unwanted weapons and Fusa snapped at him to leave the AK74 rifles out for stripping and cleaning. He then turned expectantly for his money and stared into the muzzle of the Makarov. Collins watched the man tense, then visibly relax, as they so often did when they knew that there was nothing that they could do to change the situation. Fusa closed his eyes which meant that he didn't see the muzzle flash or hear the gunshot of the bullet that killed him, entering his forehead just above the bridge of his nose. Collins fired at the back of the boy's head before he even had the chance to turn around. It wasn't the first time he had killed a child, and it probably wouldn't be the last. He swapped out the magazines and loaded two rounds into the one he had used, then pocketed the pistol, the muzzle hot against his thigh. He was fifteen thousand dollars up, and he would pick out a few of the best weapons and some ammunition to make a money and weapons cache near the border. Stewart would get the weapons they needed and would be none the wiser to what had just transpired, and Collins had just started planning for his retirement.

## Chapter Five

David arrived promptly at 8 a.m. to collect King from outside the hotel. To maintain a low profile, King settled himself in the rear seat of the vehicle as any other paying customer would. As they merged into the morning traffic, King remained vigilant, frequently checking behind them to ensure they were not being followed. The journey took them through the bustle of rush hour, first weaving through the streets of Entebbe before entering the heart of the capital, Kampala. The roads were a scene of typical chaos, crowded with an eclectic mix of bicycles, motorbikes, cars, and lorries. Here and there, cattle and donkey-drawn carts moved slowly, seemingly indifferent to the usual rules of the road and adding to the unpredictable rhythm of the city's daily commute.

After developing a sense of comfort and familiarity during their time together in the shower, King and Ginnie continued their evening by sharing a meal at the hotel restaurant. To help maintain their cover and further the impression that they were a genuine couple, they spent an additional hour in the bar, making sure to be seen together in public. Their connection led them to spend the night together, and in the morning, King quietly left Ginnie sleeping. He made his way down for an early swim, followed by breakfast beside the pool, to get into the right head space before the day's objective began. King liked Ginnie a great deal, and they had connected not only passionately but comfortably as well. Ginnie had been dating a banker for a year but felt neglected. King had been on a few dates with Jane, an intelligence officer with whom he had worked briefly with on an operation. They had not yet become intimate so he felt no guilt at what he had done with Ginnie, but he suspected that she might feel differently in the morning, so had taken the opportunity to leave early so she could at least gather her thoughts in peace. Besides, he needed to get his head in the game and get on with his work.

An hour's drive from the capital, the landscape began to transform dramatically. The terrain became increasingly hilly, with rolling elevations rising and falling across the countryside. Between these hills, broad swathes of swampland stretched out, criss-crossed by slow-moving rivers that wound their way through the many green valleys. The hills themselves were covered in lush vegetation, a testament to the region's abundant rainfall, searing summer heat, and fertile soil. Terraces had been painstakingly carved into the slopes, each one planted with crops essential to both local livelihoods and the wider economy. Rice paddies glistened in the sunlight; their roots submerged in carefully managed water channels. Coffee bushes, with their glossy leaves and ripening cherries, flourished alongside fields of sago, maize, sweet potatoes, millet, and pineapples. All these crops depended on the region's waterways, which ultimately fed into the vast expanse of Lake Victoria, sustaining both the land and its people.

David steered the vehicle off the main road, following a barely visible, overgrown access route that wound its way through the dense undergrowth. When the vehicle came to a halt, King climbed out, retrieving his change of clothes from his day sack. He slipped off his trainers, then peeled away his jeans and T-shirt until he stood in just his boxer shorts. He dressed methodically, first pulling on olive-coloured combat trousers and an olive T-shirt that fit snugly, offering both comfort and camouflage. He then laced up a pair of desert boots, sturdy and well-suited to the terrain he would be traversing. To complete his outfit, King shrugged into a lightweight tan shirt, keeping the sleeves long and the cuffs fastened. This was a deliberate choice to protect him against the sharp thorns and the notorious nettles native to the jungle, which made their European counterparts seem as harmless as aloe vera by comparison. With his new attire in place, King was ready and he folded his previous outfit and left it in the boot of the taxi. David had collected the items that Stewart had requested before King and Ginnie had left London. There was a pair of powerful Zeiss binoculars and the new Canon EOS 5D digital camera. King preferred digital cameras as he could view them in detail on the new Sony laptop that he had been given to use on the mission. The technology gave such professional results and was so user-friendly that he couldn't imagine ever using a 35mm camera again. He hung the binoculars around his neck from the strap, and checked the camera in its waterproof bag, then as he replaced it, he paid close attention to the seal and slipped it into his day sack.

King had come prepared, bringing along his trusty Swiss Army knife as a standard tool for the tasks ahead. David, recognising the need for more substantial equipment given the nature of their mission, had thoughtfully brought a machete and a KA-BAR combat knife for King's use. King examined both blades with care, finding them to be razor sharp and well suited for whatever lay ahead. After checking the blades, King secured the combat knife by fastening its sheath to his webbing belt, ensuring it was easily accessible at a moment's notice. He then took the machete, tied the rope attached to its sheath, and looped it around his neck and shoulder to keep the blade positioned across his back. The knife was for his protection from his fellow man, but the machete was a vital tool for hacking his way through the overgrowth. He could also use it to dig himself into an observation post, and he had even cooked with one before, using the blade as a makeshift skillet over hot embers for cooking foraged eggs and small game.

King checked his vintage Rolex. He had bought the watch a couple of years ago but had swapped the stainless-steel bracelet for a green NATO webbing strap. Stewart had advised him to buy the watch with his first few paycheques, not only because timing was everything in their profession, but because the timepiece was coveted enough for it to be used as currency in times that Stewart would call *when the shit hits the fan*. There was enough value in the watch on his wrist to bribe an official or buy a plane ticket out of any country. The understated timepiece, chosen as much for its reliability as its worth, served a purpose far beyond simply telling the time. In the uncertain world King operated within, possessions like this were a lifeline, an unspoken insurance policy against the unpredictable hazards of his work. Should the need arise, he could slip it from his wrist and, with a discreet exchange, secure swift passage through a checkpoint or negotiate safe exit from a hostile environment. It was a silent reassurance: a guarantee that, no matter how precarious the circumstances, there was always a way out for those who understood the unspoken currency of survival.

King checked his pack and nodded to David as he stepped into the brush. The man had been told when and where to be so there was little to be gained from telling him again and insulting his integrity. The brush was thick and after ten paces he turned around but could no longer see the taxi, although he could hear it reversing back onto the road. The ground was soft under foot, but not sodden, and the branches were low, and many covered with thorns. King knew the futility in hacking through when one could simply duck and weave and save energy. The machete weighed around five pounds, and he would soon tire if he used it on all but the thickest undergrowth. King had been in the jungle a few times before, and although he was familiar with the region's layout, marked by pockets of dense jungle interspersed with farmland and areas where the forest had once been cleared for cultivation, the terrain now felt just as impenetrable as anything he had encountered in Burundi, Angola, or the DRC. Many of the fields reclaimed from the jungle had since fallen fallow, the result of ongoing labour shortages and persistent civil unrest, allowing the thick vegetation to return and reclaim much of the landscape. As he moved forward, the dense growth closed in around him, a stark reminder of the challenges posed by the environment and the region's turbulent history.

Wary of snakes wrapped around the branches in the canopy above him that could be easily dislodged or coiled on the ground in front of him waiting to ambush prey, King tread carefully, his shirt now soaked by his perspiration and ripped along the sleeves from needle-like thorns. The gradient fell sharply, and he was aware that at the bottom of the slope would be wetlands which would present its own problems. Crocodiles, hippos, and buffalo presented a far greater danger to humans in this region than the leopards and the occasional lions that roamed the area. Yet King was fully aware that these large predators were not the only threats he might face in such an unforgiving landscape. Packs of baboons and chimpanzees, often overlooked by outsiders, were known to hunt collectively and had claimed numerous human lives across the African continent. The risks posed by wildlife, however, were only part of the equation. Equally menacing were the human dangers lurking amidst the hills. The Ugandan armed forces maintained a strong presence in the area, barracked locally and regularly conducting training exercises throughout the rugged terrain. Their vigilance was constantly heightened by the ongoing threats posed by tribal factions, criminal gangs, and rebel groups operating in the vicinity. In addition to these internal challenges, there was always the looming possibility of incursions by insurgents crossing over from the neighbouring countries of the DRC and Rwanda, adding another layer of unpredictability and peril to the environment King was navigating.

King eventually reached the point where ducking and weaving would no longer suffice. He removed the machete from across his back and set to work on the tangled vines obstructing his path. The vines were thick, some as wide as his wrist, and tightly interwoven, forming a near-impenetrable barrier. With each swing, the machete bit into the living green, the dense growth resisting before finally yielding. Twenty minutes passed in this arduous fashion, sweat running down his back and his arms aching from the repetitive effort. At last, his persistence paid off. The final tangle of vines gave way, and King stumbled through the gap he had carved, emerging into a sudden clearing. Pausing to catch his breath, King reached for one of the six plastic bottles of French mineral water he had brought along, purchased from the hotel bar the previous evening. He took a long drink, letting the cool liquid soothe his parched throat, before recapping the bottle and steeling himself for what lay ahead. He pressed forward, crossing the small clearing that marked the edge of the dense brush. With careful strokes, he began hacking at the barrier of stubborn thorns, each swing of the machete opening the way by only a fraction. The tangle of vegetation resisted, but after several determined cuts, the wall of foliage abruptly cleared. King nearly lost his balance, stumbling forward as the undergrowth parted. In an instant, the oppressive green of the jungle was replaced by the open expanse of cultivated land. The shift was so abrupt, so strangely concealed until the very last moment, that for a few seconds, King struggled to accept it as reality. The world on the other side of the thorns was ordered and familiar, rows of crops stretching away from him, standing in stark contrast to the wild, unkempt chaos of the jungle behind.

As King moved forward, his gaze swept across the marshland that lay just beyond the cultivated fields. The gentle flow of the river traced its way through the landscape, while terraces of sago rose in neat succession up the side of a distant hill, resembling a giant staircase carved into the earth. It was clear to King that the plantation sat approximately midway up the hillside, but his objective required more than a passing glance from below. To establish a suitable surveillance position—known in his training as a 'laying up place' or LUP—King knew he needed to secure the high ground. Only from that vantage point could he effectively observe both the plantation and its surroundings, remaining concealed yet alert to any developments.

## Crossfire

Glancing at his watch, King attempted to estimate how long it would take to reach the summit. He was aware, however, that the route ahead was riddled with uncertainties: the unpredictable terrain, the marshland, dangerous game and any unforeseen obstacles that might slow his progress. Undeterred by these variables, King pressed onwards, carefully skirting the edge of the field until he arrived at the marshland, ready to tackle the next challenge on his path towards the ideal observation point.

King cut a straight branch as he reached the swamp and whittled off the twigs and leaves. The pole that he was left with measured around two metres in length, and he used it to probe the depth of the swamp, stepping into the knee-deep water that was as black as coal. The ooze underfoot was thick, a mulch of mud and leaves and rotten branches that gave under his weight. He sheathed the machete and used both hands to steady himself, using the pole both to probe the depth and to aid his balance. He made steady progress, his eyes darting everywhere. Crocodiles, he knew, could be lying just beneath the surface of the water, concealed and waiting for the slightest sign of movement, ever eager for an easy meal. Yet, despite the threat they posed, it was the hippos that filled him with the greatest apprehension. While a well-armed man might stand a chance against a crocodile, perhaps even fighting it off with a machete or a staff if caught unawares, hippos were another matter entirely. Their sheer size, speed, and aggression made them far more dangerous in close quarters. From all accounts, the only people who ever survived a hippo attack were those fortunate enough that the animal simply lost interest and moved on. The odds of fending off such a powerful creature were practically non-existent, and King was acutely aware that luck played a far greater role in such encounters than any amount of preparation or weaponry could offer.

After a hundred metres or so, the swamp met the river and King studied the water in both directions, paying close attention to the opposite riverbank. He was looking for the telltale signs of crocodiles – claw marks and tracks, belly indents where they slid through the mud to reach the water. King was sure that he could not see any and he took a deep breath to ready himself for the swim. It wasn't far, barely twenty metres, but he had to decide whether to go for it and sprint in a strong front crawl or slip gently into the water and try a slow and steady breaststroke with minimal splash. He decided on stealth because he may well make it across but if he drew crocodiles because of the splash, then they may remain in the area which would be problematic upon his return. The water was cooler than the air temperature and he was grateful to wash the perspiration off him as he set out in a steady breaststroke. He pushed thoughts of what could be swimming beneath him in the depths and kept his eyes on the surface all around him and the opposite bank. So far, so good. King suffered a jump-scare when his right foot touched the riverbed, but reasoning kicked in and he touched down with both feet and waded through the water which rapidly became shallow and he was soon standing in ankle-deep mud. He made his way quickly up the riverbank and did not hesitate to step into the undergrowth rather than remain exposed.

King unslung the machete and stripped off the shirt and T-shirt, wringing them out by twisting them around a thin branch until barely a drip leached out. He hung the shirt on a branch and put the T-shirt back on before kicking off his boots and wringing out his socks. He repeated the process with his trousers and boxers and dressed hurriedly, putting the shirt on last. He drank an entire bottle of water and put the empty bottle back in his pack. He had been on the move for two hours and he was hungry. He ate one of six packets of roasted peanuts that he had bought with the water from the hotel bar and washed them down with most of another bottle of water. With salt, sugar and water on board, he felt replenished and ready for the climb that would take him above the plantation and to his objective.

# Chapter Six

Collins tossed the shovel into the rear of the Toyota Landcruiser and looked at the area of ground in front of him. He had buried the crate two-feet down and after he had filled in the soil, he had sprinkled leaf litter and branches over the disturbed earth. He was confident that it would remain undiscovered for all eternity, such was the remoteness of the location. He had marked the spot with GPS coordinates and was confident that he could find the spot even without a GPS handset. Inside the crate were three Heckler & Koch rifles, two Browning pistols, and magazines and ammunition for both along with ten thousand dollars in used banknotes. It was the third and final cache that he had dug along the border, and they would provide him with money, protection, or even revenue when the shit hit the fan. He now had twenty of these caches spread across three continents and a dozen countries. Collins was preparing for a rainy day, in a profession where it could suddenly start pissing down.

Collins drove out of the clearing and along the farm track back to the road and after a couple of miles he stopped beside a river and put the vehicle into park. He waited and listened with the window open, then when he was sure that all he could hear was the sound of the engine ticking cool, he got out and opened the tailgate. The crates that he had 'purchased' from Fusa were still there, but he took the shovel before looking around and then tossing it into the river. He had been sent to procure weapons and did not want to be forced to explain why he had bought a shovel at an ironmonger. It was all Peter Stewart's fault, of course. He continued to champion King, and he had never truly felt part of the team. King had screwed up a mission involving an organised crime gang and the IRA, and he had been lucky to redeem himself. Collins did not know the details, but King had lost an asset and a great deal of money. The bad guys had been killed and a rogue MI6 officer exposed, but the operation had been tainted. King had made up for his shortcomings on two jobs in Africa, where had carried Stewart on his back after being injured on the last operation, refusing to allow the man to die in the field. Stewart owed the man his life, and Collins knew that he would be lucky to get a line of credit as strong as that, and now he had the debacle that was Beirut blotting his copybook. There was little more he could do, and he had started to plan for his exit. He had honed his skills and made valuable contacts, and he realised that there were people who would pay a great deal for his services.

Collins started the Landcruiser, then took his phone out from his pocket when the silent alert vibrated against his leg.

"Yes?" he said curtly.

"Have you thought about my offer?"

"I have."

"Well?"

"I'll do it."

"Where are you?"

"Funny you should ask," he said lightly. "Tanzania."

"It's karma, then."

"I think it's kismet," Collins replied.

"What's the fucking difference, bru?"

"One's paid forward, the other is payback."

"I can be there in..." There was a long pause, and Collins could hear keyboard keys tapping and the man clicking a computer mouse. "Oh, fuck... it's two stops from Cape Town... Kilimanjaro International in fifteen hours... Let's make it twenty-four hours. I'll text you with the name of my hotel and we'll have some beers and steaks and talk about your future."

"Okay, bru," Collins replied, and ended the call. *Fuck King and fuck that alcoholic Scotsman,* he thought. He was damned if he was going to be the errand boy and go out and buy guns while King did the recon and planning. He was every bit as good as King, if not better. It was time to go it alone and make some real money instead of a civil servant's salary. But first, he would see that the craggy, old Scottish bastard got his guns, and so much more besides.

## Chapter Seven

King had managed to complete the climb within an hour. The journey was largely uneventful, with only a handful of animal encounters along the way. He spotted several snakes slithering silently into the thick undergrowth, their movements quick and unobtrusive. At times, he had to navigate carefully to avoid walking straight into sizeable spiderwebs strung between branches, their delicate strands almost invisible in the dappled light. Aside from these minor encounters, the only other signs of life were birds startled by his approach. As King drew near, flurries of wings erupted from the trees, the birds taking flight and vanishing into the forest canopy. Despite his initial apprehension, none of his fears came to pass during the ascent.

The plantation could be reached via a gravelled road that led in from the east. According to King's initial intelligence report, the main activity on the estate involved harvesting and distributing coffee beans, with operations focused primarily on the far side of the hill. The hillside from which King had made his approach remained untouched, neither cleared nor cultivated, suggesting that the plantation's expansion had not yet reached that area.

King selected a concealed spot along the hillside, using his machete to dig out a shallow depression in the earth. He lined the pit with fronds taken from nearby small palms, creating a makeshift bed to lie upon that would both cushion him and keep him dry from the damp earth. In front of his position, he scraped together a low mound of soil, shaping it as a rest that would support his binoculars while he observed the plantation below. To further improve his concealment, King methodically cut branches from the surrounding foliage and laid them in front of him, ensuring he was well hidden from any prying eyes. He carefully parted the dense greenery, cutting down certain plants and bending others aside, crossing them to keep his line of sight clear. With his hide prepared, King settled into position, took a steady drink from his water supply, and ate a few more handfuls of nuts to keep his energy up as he began his surveillance of the plantation.

## Chapter Eight
### Kenya

Peter Stewart observed as the two aged Land Rovers made their way along the meandering dirt track. As they travelled, large plumes of dust rose up behind them, drifting into the air and marking their passage through the otherwise tranquil landscape. The vehicles were equipped with canvas sides, yet these had been rolled up and secured, providing the men seated in the rear with some respite from the oppressive heat. The simple act of fastening the canvas allowed the breeze to circulate freely, offering a welcome relief as the convoy pressed on through the rugged terrain.

He took one last swig of Scotch from the quarter bottle that he had purchased in the duty free at the airport, savouring it, turning the bottle in his hand as it picked up the light. The amber liquid glinted, casting shifting patterns across the table as he contemplated the day's events. He shrugged as he decided to finish the bottle. Each sip was measured and slow, the taste lingering on his tongue, its warmth spreading through him. He paused, listening to the quiet around him, letting the moment settle before the next step in his journey. The ritual of drinking alone, reflecting in silence, offered a brief respite before he would have to face the uncertainty that lay ahead. Because now he would not drink properly until the end of the mission, and he just prayed that he lived to take another drink. Some soldiers prayed to live so they could see their loved ones again, others prayed that they would hold their nerve in battle and not die disgraced, but Stewart only hoped to stay alive to break the seal on a bottle of fine Scotch.

Both vehicles entered the compound and stopped. Six men jumped out of the first truck, while two from the second unloaded crates, boxes, and bottled water. The second driver switched to the first vehicle, which then exited the compound. Stewart thought the delivery seamless and was only too glad that he did not have anything to do with the drivers. He just hoped that they had left the keys in the ignition as instructed.

"Peter, yer old dog!" a tough-looking Irishman shouted. He had a mane of light brown hair and a thick beard that was red but speckled with grey.

"Paddy..." Stewart grinned as he walked up to the four men. "How are you, yer big Mick?" He shook the man's hand warmly and patted him on the shoulder.

"Aye, still breathing," he replied. "This is Josh," he said, nodding to a tanned man a decade younger than himself with a crew cut and tattooed arms. "As I said, he's a good man..."

"Good to meet you, Josh," Stewart shook the man's hand, then turned to a black man in his early thirties. "And good to see you again, Chris."

"Major..." Chris nodded, using the rank Stewart had held in the SAS before leaving for MI6. He had moved to

London from Jamaica as a child and still had a strong Jamaican accent and often slipped into Patois

Stewart had first noticed Chris Cargill in the Parachute Regiment and had invited the man to join SAS selection. Tough and wiry, he was an accomplished gymnast and had excelled in CRW – Counter Revolutionary Warfare – and was everybody's first choice to be first man in whether it was using a ladder or abseiling through a window. Stewart had always joked that you could shoot the fella out of a circus cannon, and he'd still make it through the window.

Stewart did not know the last man, but he had been recommended by someone he used to serve with and trusted implicitly, so that was good enough for him. Besides, the training he had planned would show everybody's strength and weaknesses soon enough. "Peter Stewart," he remarked, holding out his hand.

The man gripped it firmly and said, "Sam..." Offering no surname. Stewart would not ask, either. Mercenary work often meant that your last comrade was your next enemy, and everyone respected a man's desire for privacy.

"You've got your work cut out today," said Stewart. "The compound is used by the Kenyan army but was overrun by Al-Shabaab earlier this year. The Kenyans will come back to use it but are still licking their wounds for now. The upshot is we have the place to ourselves and are unlikely to be interrupted. The downside is the Islamist extremists torched the place and for some reason known only to themselves, they smashed up the toilets because they prefer to shit in a hole in the ground." Stewart paused. "So, we have been dragged down to their level. Sort it out amongst yourselves, but we need latrines dug out, somewhere to cook and something to cook on, and somewhere to bed down for a few nights."

"I've been paid to fight, not dig latrines or set up camp," Josh stated flatly.

"Wind yer fecking neck in, lad," Paddy snapped. "I've fecking well vouched for you..."

"You've been paid to soldier," Stewart replied. "And the last time I fucking checked that meant securing your base and getting a fucking brew on." He paused. "Anyway, we haven't got the weapons yet, so until then we fix a place to eat and sleep and get some physical in..."

Josh shrugged but didn't reply.

"Yer fecking tit..." Paddy muttered under his breath.

"I'll dig the shitter," said Chris. "I don't trust you fuckers to dig it deep enough and don't want my dick to touch the bottom when I squat..."

There was laughter all round and Stewart walked off shaking his head but pleased that Chris had moved on the conversation and eased the tension, although he would watch Josh closely from now on.

Chris selected a spade and a pick from the collection of tools abandoned by the Kenyans. Without a word, he set off at a brisk pace, putting a respectable fifty metres between himself and the main compound before beginning to dig the latrines. His choice of location and willingness to take on the unpleasant task earned him a measure of respect from the others. Meanwhile, Josh and Paddy worked together to remove scorched planks of wood from the building. Using jemmy bars, they prised the charred timbers loose and systematically stacked them in a neat pile. These materials would later be repurposed for construction around the camp, demonstrating a practical approach to making use of what little was available. At the same time, Sam took it upon himself to collect several oil drums, rolling them carefully over to the growing pile of salvaged materials. The drums, like the wood, were earmarked for further use in building makeshift cooking facilities or other essential structures required to sustain the group for the nights ahead.

Stewart organised a fire and watched the men work through the problems. He knew that Paddy was a fearsome warrior, but he liked to have clear orders. There was nothing wrong in that, some men were never meant to be generals. Despite Josh's earlier lack of enthusiasm for manual work, he had got stuck into the tasks, although he suspected that Paddy was motivating him, and the younger man had realised his mistake. It was a new group, and Stewart knew that in new groups someone usually fucked up early on. He supposed that Josh had merely got there first.

By the time Stewart had brewed five tin mugs of tea with powdered milk, the men had fashioned a bunk area with a lean-to roof, and an oil drum had been cut in half with a hacksaw and wedged up on blocks to make a cooking pit. Wood was now burning fiercely, and someone had taken the bars from one of the burned down huts and wedged it into the oil drum to make a grill.

Chris's choice of location for the latrine ensured it was positioned at a sufficient distance from the main compound, affording users a degree of privacy while also maintaining basic hygiene standards. Once the latrine was established, the team turned their attention to personal cleanliness. Ingeniously, they crafted a makeshift shower using a bucket and the natural resources at hand. A sturdy branch from one of several papaya trees, planted within the compound not only for their shade but also as a source of food, served as the support for the shower. The bucket was hung by its handle at a height of around seven feet above the ground. To allow for controlled water flow, a hole was bored through the bucket near the handle, through which a short length of rope was threaded and secured. This simple mechanism meant that any user could stand beneath the bucket and, by gently pulling on the rope, tip water from the bucket over themselves, creating a rudimentary yet functional shower. Stewart dubbed this contraption a "Scottish shower", though no one thought to ask him the reason behind the name.

It was getting late so Josh and Paddy cooked some rice and beans and opened some tins of corned beef and between them rustled up something quite disgusting. They ate from mess tins and drank strong tea and talked around the fire like men had done before battle for thousands of years. Stewart leaned back listening to the men as they got to know each other and tentatively talked about previous jobs they had done around the world without giving too much away. Mercenaries walked a fine line, and it was quite possible for men on a job to have previously fought on opposing sides. Comrades in arms one moment, enemies the next. Stewart had been a professional soldier since the tender age of sixteen. He had served in the British army and the SAS, then fought private wars for MI6. He had been around long enough for his government to send him to battle against a regime or country, and then for that country when alliances and allegiances changed with political will, so he preferred at times like this, to keep his mouth shut. If he had killed the best friend of one of these men, then he wouldn't like to stand in front of them when they had a loaded gun in their hand.

## Chapter Nine
### Uganda

Farm workers came and went, and the few soldiers guarding the plantation smoked and joked and lounged about until midday when they sought shade and something to eat. King watched throughout the afternoon, taking pictures and making notes in his own shorthand. After six hours laying prone, he tensed when he saw the prisoners being walked around the gardens. He switched to the camera and wasn't shy about using the SD card's memory. Another win for the digital camera over the normal thirty-six shots that a 35mm would have allowed. Not to mention the fiddly film change. King went through the photographs using the camera's display window, zooming in on the faces. It was a hard call, and he was ashamed that he thought the men looked the same as one another, but they all sported a grade one crew cut and looked to be around the same weight. There were a few skin tones that he could rule out immediately, but he imagined that Stewart may have to engage the skills of some of the analysts and their facial recognition software where they worked in the basement of the River House. Two more soldiers left the plantation house either side of a prisoner and it suddenly hit King that this was his man. Moffusa Bentuwi carried himself with poise and dignity that was not evident in the other prisoners. The rightful elected President of Uganda under 'house arrest' for inciting insurrection, for threatening change. Pending a trial that would never come, and a plight that much of the world had either forgotten or found inconvenient to champion.

King wondered what the other political prisoners had done, what their perceived crimes had been. He watched as Bentuwi was accompanied around the garden, never less than fifty feet from another prisoner, but where the other six men seemed to be given the freedom of walking around with three guards watching nearby, Moffusa Bentuwi was shadowed constantly. King switched to the more powerful binoculars and noted the weaponry of the soldiers. It was a mixed bag of FN FAL, Kalashnikov AK74 and AK47 rifles, and Uzi machine pistols. None of the men carried a pistol, and they all seemed to have just one or two spare magazines tucked into their breast pockets. These men were not prepared for war. King used several markers to ascertain the distance by ball-parking the tallest of the men at six feet in height. A few inches in height was neither here nor there, but it gave him a distance of approximately five hundred metres. He did not yet know what weapons Collins had procured, but it would make sense to have a man in an overwatch position with a SAW, or Squad Automatic Weapon, something like an M60 or a GPMG. Then, he would have deployed a sniper with a powerful rifle and a well-zeroed scope, who could do a lot of damage from King's current position.

King watched as Bentuwi was escorted back inside the plantation house. The other prisoners were taken in last,

## Crossfire

and twenty minutes later the five soldiers came back outside and took a break on one of the lawns. Stewart's first piece of intelligence had proven correct. Moffusa Bentuwi was on site. That was miracle number one. Now they had to work out how to lift him. That, and how to kill one of the most barbaric and military leaders on the African continent and remove the current President from office.

# Chapter Ten

King stood by the edge of the slow-moving river, carefully observing its surface. The warmth of the sun pressed reassuringly against his back, a small comfort as he focused intently on the water before him. He was grateful that the sun's position meant he did not have to squint or shield his eyes from any glare, allowing him to concentrate fully on what lay ahead. His focus soon paid off. In the middle of the river, almost perfectly camouflaged, a crocodile lingered. It was a formidable creature, at least four metres long, with only its nostrils visible above the water, betraying its presence. The crocodile had already noticed King, likely from the moment he had emerged through the thick undergrowth, still a good dozen metres from the riverbank. The realisation sent King's heart pounding. He was acutely aware of how dangerous it would be to underestimate such a predator or to make a mistake with it lurking just beneath the surface.

He remembered a survival expert explaining the difference between sharks and crocodiles and it had always stuck with him. If a person swam in the sea a hundred times in

## Crossfire

their lifetime, then they had probably shared a dozen of their swims with a shark. By contrast, if a crocodile was in your vicinity when you swam then you would know it because you would be attacked. If you swam and were not attacked, then a crocodile had never been close enough to you to begin with. King had never truly known whether the man had been serious, but he had taken the man's point.

King stepped back a few paces from the water's edge and turned his attention upriver. He watched for a few minutes, satisfied that there were no more crocodiles sunning themselves on the riverbanks. He looked back at the crocodile, its nostrils creating little eddies as the water flowed around them, the creature moving its tail almost imperceivably to maintain its position in front of King. Downriver, the story was the same. No movement on the banks, until a small gazelle, no larger than a whippet picked its way down the muddy riverbank and looked about itself. King remain stock-still, his eyes fixed on the tiny creature as it shivered and ticked, reacting to hungry, troublesome flies. King looked back at the water in front of him, but the beast was no longer there.

King watched the tiny gazelle as it tentatively bowed its head and started to drink. Naturally wary, the creature lifted its head, frozen to the spot as it listened and waited for movement. King remained still. Dressed in tan and olive, and covered in mud, he blended into the landscape, the foliage behind him and the sun in the gazelle's eyes. King flinched as the crocodile drove itself out of the water all the way to its tail, its great jaws clamping around the gazelle, the poor creature's head and neck snagged in the beast's vice-like grip. The crocodile dropped back into the water, only its head and neck could be seen, and it raised its head, the gazelle lifted completely before the great beast started its death roll, and King could hear the snapping of bones above the splashing of water.

King looked back at the water in front of him, the sunlight penetrating just enough to allow him to see a few feet below the surface—this had been the reason he had spotted the crocodile in the first place. Without hesitation, he dived in, stroking hard beneath the surface, moving as quickly and powerfully as he could. As he broke through the water's surface, he pumped his arms and kicked his legs with all his strength, not pausing to breathe between strokes. He simply held his breath, single-mindedly focused on reaching the safety of the shallows. Scrambling through the shallow water, King continued onwards until he reached the riverbank. Only once he was safely on solid ground did he allow himself to look back at the river. There, either the same crocodile or an equally large companion thrashed violently through the water, abandoning its pursuit now that its intended prey was too far from the river's edge to attack. It had been close, and King had been completely unaware.

King's heart continued to pound in his chest, the adrenaline from his close encounter with the crocodile lingering as he pressed on. Not willing to let his guard down for even a moment, he carefully picked his way through the long grass that bordered the riverbank. Each step was measured and deliberate, his senses straining for any sign of danger hidden within the thick undergrowth. As he reached the edge of the swamp, the ground grew softer underfoot, and soon he found himself wading into knee-deep water. The mud sucked at his boots, making every movement a labour. He realised with a pang of annoyance that he had forgotten to retrieve the sturdy pole he had cut for himself earlier—a valuable tool for testing the treacherous ground ahead.

## Crossfire

Forced to improvise, King drew his machete, gripping it tightly. He used the blade to prod the murky water before each step, wary of hidden threats lurking beneath the surface. Crocodile territory demanded constant vigilance. King's eyes darted from shadow to ripple, his mind racing through every lesson and warning he had ever heard about the perils of the African swamps. He knew he could not allow himself to relax, not even for a moment, until he was safely across. Just one hundred metres separated him from the relative safety of the cultivated land beyond, but each metre felt like a mile as he inched his way forward, alert to every possible danger.

King stayed along the farmland's edge, relaxing only when he reached the cover of the jungle. The sun was setting behind him, and the jungle was eerily dark. Instinctively, he crouched at the sound, eyes fixed on the direction of the snapping of branches and voices. He smelled cigarette smoke before he saw the two men, emerging one at a time from the dense foliage just a few metres in front of him. King's grip tightened on the machete as he saw the rifles hanging from their shoulders. He had nowhere to go, with only a low branch affording him cover. If he had a gun, then he would have dropped them both, but that would mean that somewhere in the chain, the alarm would be raised, and he would have lost the element of surprise. Either a reaction to the gunshot, or when the soldiers failed to return from their patrol. But who the hell mounted a two-man patrol, anyway? King got his answer when they rested their rifles on a tree. Then, one of the men undid his trousers and the other man got down onto his knees. King couldn't move, and he was damned if he wanted to bear witness to an illicit jungle frolic, but he was faced with little choice. Uganda still imposed the death penalty for homosexuals, and these two weren't taking any chances in being seen.

King would have closed his eyes if he could, but soldiers were soldiers, and the rifles were closer to them than King was, so he could not afford to let down his guard for a second. The man still standing rolled his head pleasurably, his eyes wide, then froze when he stared straight into King's eyes. King sprang to his feet as both men stared at him, then went for the rifles. The man with his trousers around his ankles was slow and hampered by his situation, and King brought the machete down on the man's shoulder. He drew the knife as the man screamed and fell to his knees and sliced him across the throat as he passed him, on a direct attack towards the other man who had reached his FN FAL rifle. The man swung the weapon around, but King swung the machete and the blade clattered against the barrel and as it glanced away he plunged the knife deep into the man's throat.

The man released his grip on the rifle and King stood back, looking away somewhat awkwardly, as the two men died. It felt like the ultimate invasion of the soul, watching someone die by your hand.

When both men had finally bled out, their arms and legs rested eerily still. He had used the time to assess his situation, and he now had formulated the bare bones of a plan. He could not leave the bodies where they were for fear of discovery, and even if he dug shallow graves then predators would have them uncovered by morning. Which left the unthinkable.

King went to work. He pulled up and fastened the man's trousers and hauled the dead weight, leaning the body back against a branch. He then lifted the other body, which was thankfully at least a stone lighter, and found a

## Crossfire

low branch where he could prop up the corpse. He was already out of breath from the fight and adrenalin release, but he picked up both weapons and slung them around his neck by the canvas slings. The FN FAL battle rifle was a heavy beast, around ten pounds loaded, and he bent down and positioned the heavier body over his right shoulder and shifted the weight until it was comfortable and balanced, then he squat down and pulled the other body over his left shoulder and stood up. King lifted weights most days and performed two-hundred press-ups and sit-ups daily, along with daily runs, but as he broke free of the undergrowth and out into the fields, he knew that he had an arduous task ahead of him.

By the time King reached the swamp, fatigue had taken its toll. He dropped the heavier of the two bodies onto the sodden ground, pausing to catch his breath. With practicality in mind, he unslung one of the rifles, intending to use it as a makeshift probe to test the water's depth before proceeding. He had barely advanced a few steps into the murky terrain when a sudden thrashing noise in front of him brought him to an abrupt halt. Through the dim light, King could make out the formidable shape of a crocodile lurking ahead, its head raised menacingly and jaws wide open. The creature's emerald eyes gleamed, reflecting the faint moonlight that filtered through the shifting clouds above. Assessing the danger, King quickly slung the body between himself and the crocodile, then retreated several steps.

King heaved the second stiffening body onto his shoulder and made it halfway through the swamp when he saw more crocodiles ripping at the corpse, and smaller crocodiles swimming through the shallows from the river as they joined the feeding frenzy. King got as close as he dared, and heaved the body forwards, where it splashed filthy water over him. He stepped backwards, his eyes darting around him for fear of being cut off from dry land, then when he was close to the edge of the swamp, he threw both rifles as far as he could towards the thrashing water.

Exhausted, he trudged back around the edge of the fields and into the pitch-black jungle. He collected his pack and used a pen torch with a red filter to illuminate his path, checking the button compass hanging around his neck underneath his T-shirt for his bearings. He was over an hour late for his rendezvous with David and the welcoming comfort of the taxi, and just hoped upon all hope that the man had waited.

# Chapter Eleven
## Kenya

Stewart stood on the edge of the landing strip; his gaze fixed intently on the incoming Piper twin-prop airplane. A limp windsock hanging from a rusty pole indicated that the air was still and it would be a harsh landing. As the aircraft descended, its wheels touched the dusty strip, raising plumes of powdery, red earth into the air. The plane bounced unevenly on its three tyres, the shocks absorbing the rough ground as it made several brief hops before finally settling. Once steady, the pilot eased back on the throttle and applied the brakes, bringing the small aircraft to a gradual halt amidst the swirling dust.

Paddy drove the Land Rover with Josh riding up front, and Chris and Sam in the rear. The pilot had exited the aircraft by the time they reached him and the two men hopped out of the back of the Land Rover and started to unload the crates. Stewart had given Paddy the second half of the pilot's fee and was counting it out in front of him. No refreshments were offered, and this was as close as the pilot would get to the camp, which suited both parties. In this line of work, it never paid to know too much about something that did not concern you. Richard Collins had paid the pilot his initial fee, with the second half payable upon delivery. You never wanted to pay the full fee upfront in this game, either.

With the exchange finalised, the group climbed back into the Land Rover. As they set off towards the compound, the pilot wasted no time in preparing for departure. Having already turned the aircraft around, he made use of the full length of the gravelled runway, trying to make up for the absence of a headwind that would normally assist with generating the lift needed for take-off. The vehicle rumbled away from the airstrip, leaving swirling dust in its wake as the plane gathered speed behind them, engines labouring against the still air in an effort to achieve flight.

"Break out the toys, lads," Stewart said as the men got out of the vehicle.

The men had constructed a makeshift firing range, positioning targets at distances of fifty, one hundred, and two hundred metres. This allowed for initial zeroing of their weapons as well as thorough testing. In addition to the outdoor range, the group worked together to clear debris from the fire-damaged barracks, creating suitable spaces to set up targets for practising room clearing scenarios. All four men were experienced professionals, each bringing a background in the mercenary business, though none chose to discuss their most recent assignments. Stewart, recognising the importance of readiness, ensured that every member was armed and took part in a series of drills. These exercises served a dual purpose: sharpening their individual and collective skills, while also providing Stewart the opportunity to assess the strengths and weaknesses within the group.

They had awoken at five-thirty and breakfasted on

strong, black coffee, sweet long-life bread, fried spam and boiled eggs. Again, quite a disgusting meal, and if strengths and weaknesses were to be judged on every action, then Paddy and Josh should not be allowed near food preparation ever again. PT followed, with a five-miler where two of the men saw their breakfast for a second time, with Chris reporting to the two cooks that it tasted better on the way out. Circuit training repetitions of press-ups, sit-ups, burpees and squats preceded a barrel race where the men ran a two-man relay over one hundred metres carrying empty forty-five-gallon oil drums. Once the men had taken turns to carry one another over a five hundred metre trek through the bush, Stewart had called time and prepared for the delivery of weapons.

The men were fit and well-motivated and he did not see the need to beast them again. They would run through a detailed marksmanship and weapon handling practice, then go out into the bush in pairs to find something tastier to eat than long-life bread and warm tinned mystery meat.

Paddy jemmied the lids of the crates, and the men laid the weapons out on the ground on top of a large ground sheet.

"Put the ammo for the operation to one side," said Stewart to nobody, although he watched who reacted first to the order. "Two magazines worth of nine-millimetre and two hundred rounds each of seven-six-two for the rifles. Seven men in all."

"Who else is coming?" asked Sam.

"Need to know, pal," Paddy said.

"Aye, and you don't need to know just yet," Stewart remarked flatly.

Sam shrugged and continued to stack the cardboard cartons of ammunition to one side.

"Everything else is for practice," said Stewart. "And save a few rounds for some bush meat. We're barbecuing from now on." He paused. "I'm not eating anything else cooked by the Roux Brothers, here..."

The men burst into laughter, the camaraderie evident as Paddy, grinning broadly, directed a light-hearted jibe at Stewart, telling him in no uncertain terms what he could do to himself. Stewart took the comment in his stride, his smile betraying his satisfaction. The exchange was more than just banter; it was a sign that the group was beginning to bond in earnest. In these moments of shared humour and mutual respect, Stewart could see the foundations of a solid team taking shape, and he found himself genuinely pleased with the progress they were making together.

## Chapter Twelve

King smiled to himself when he thought of last night, the memory warm and delicious in the stark contrast to his current surroundings. He had arrived back at the hotel at 9 p.m. and showered the dirt and death and memory from him. He had hung his filthy clothes on the balcony, the outflow of the air conditioning unit as good as any radiator. He had not washed them because the jungle smelled of decay, not peach shower gel, and he would be in the wilds again tomorrow. He had changed into a pair of thin beige tropical trousers and a loose-fitting white linen shirt and had joined Ginnie in the bar for a cold beer and to decompress. Ginnie had read a trashy novel on the balcony, taken a few swims and hit the room service menu. It didn't make for the most interesting holiday, but she had said that it felt like heaven compared to being couped up in her office at the River House with an inbox that always seemed ten times higher than her outbox.

They had eaten a good meal in the restaurant and taken drinks beside the pool, the gardens alive with crickets and croaking frogs in the reeds of the water features, with the sound of running water adding some background harmony to nature's chorus. The mutual comfort between them gave way to sexual tension and they retired to the room shortly before midnight. Ginnie had forgotten all about her boyfriend with the attention issues, and King had given up thinking about another date with Jane, and afterwards they had finally fallen asleep after three. King had once again left Ginnie sleeping and had woken himself up with a short swim at seven and eaten a light breakfast. He was inside David's taxi shortly before eight and by ten, King was alone again in the bush, fifty miles west from yesterday's reconnaissance.

The terrain presented a marked contrast to the previous day's stakeout of the plantation, which had been used to detain prisoners deemed politically significant. Here, the Rwenzori Mountains loomed, rising to a formidable height of five thousand metres above sea level. The military compound was situated roughly halfway up the mountains, perched on a broad plateau at an altitude of three thousand feet. Its proximity to the border with the Democratic Republic of Congo made it a crucial strategic position—a forward operating base established to counter incursions from marauding gangs, local tribes and various armed factions. The setting was remote and rugged, underscoring both the isolation and the significance of the outpost.

King was acutely aware of the dangers lurking in the waterways scattered throughout the foothills. The presence of crocodiles was known, although he suspected their numbers would diminish as he ascended further up the slopes. David had warned him about leopards and baboons, cautioning him to remain vigilant for venomous snakes and formidable rock pythons. Despite these natural threats, King's primary concern lay elsewhere. The slopes were regularly patrolled by soldiers, and he understood that every step closer to the military compound would only increase the peril. The risks were mounting, with the tension rising as he pressed on towards his destination.

King had been trekking through the rugged terrain for about an hour when he spotted a military patrol in the distance. The sight immediately heightened his sense of alertness. He carried the camera for documenting his journey, and the pair of Zeiss binoculars securely fastened around his neck, ready to be used at a moment's notice. Although the machete he brought with him was less critical in this landscape, its presence offered a reassuring sense of security in such a potentially hostile environment. The knife was a vital piece of equipment in King's kit. Its utility extended well beyond self-defence; it was indispensable for bushcraft. With the knife, King could cut tinder and kindling to start fires, using the magnesium stick attached to its sheath to create a spark. Additionally, the knife served a variety of other purposes—digging, hunting, and preparing food—making it an essential tool for survival in the wild. However, he was confident that MI6's intelligence was good and accurate, and he would hopefully sleep again tonight in his hotel bed. The thought of Ginnie being there suddenly warmed his soul, comforting him, and he had to admit that he was falling for her.

Within his backpack, King carried a guidebook detailing the bird species of Africa alongside a journal. The journal contained his handwritten notes and sketches of various birds, created during his flight from London to Entebbe Airport. By removing the shorthand pages that documented his observations from the previous day's reconnaissance, King ensured that his belongings would reinforce his cover story. Should he be stopped and questioned, the absence of sensitive material and the presence of birdwatching literature would help support his claim of being a freelance nature journalist, enabling him to plausibly talk his way out of any compromising situation.

King remained perfectly still as he surveyed the approaching soldiers, acutely aware that any sudden movement could easily betray his position. He understood that, in situations like these, even the slightest misstep could draw unwanted attention. Carefully, he lowered himself to the ground, keeping his actions slow and deliberate so as not to attract notice. His focus remained fixed on the patrol, counting twenty men in total. The unit was situated approximately four hundred metres away, making their way across the slope from east to west. Their direction of travel indicated that they were heading towards the border with the Democratic Republic of Congo, a detail King noted as he assessed the potential risk of discovery. Deciding to document the scene, King switched to his camera and discreetly took a few shots of the patrol. He was mindful of the consequences should any member of the group become aware of his presence; if it appeared that they might move to intercept him, he was prepared to delete the images immediately, ensuring no evidence remained. Fortunately, he had already replaced his old SD card with a new one back at the hotel, meaning he was not carrying any other potentially incriminating material with him.

His phone vibrated in his pocket, and he cursed as he concentrated on the patrol. Each man was armed with a FN FAL as their primary weapon, and they carried plenty of magazines in bandoliers. One of the men carried a GPMG that looked like an American M60 - a chain-fed machinegun used for sustained or covering fire – while the ammunition boxes had been shared among six of the troops.

**Crossfire**

King could see two RPGs, and no doubt many of the men would be carrying a rocket in their packs. There was a lot of firepower and if they were indeed to assassinate General Mantutsi, then they could not kid themselves that it was going to be easy getting away afterwards.

When the patrol disappeared around the mountainside, King relaxed, taking a deep breath as he took out his phone and checked the screen.

*Got to leave now. Sorry, orders. It's been nice x*

King frowned, feeling a twist in his guts. So, that was it. A brief affair and she was gone. No doubt, she'd be pick up where she had left off with her banker boyfriend in The City, business as usual. King probably wouldn't even see her again, and the thought just didn't sit right with him, and he couldn't help feeling regret that their last embrace, really would be the last time he held her.

## Chapter Thirteen
### Tanzania

Collins sipped a cold beer watching the late afternoon sun glisten on the still waters of Lake Victoria. The bar was quiet, and the waitress was sitting at the next table, her breasts and arms resting on the table with her head turned sideways. She was sleeping soundly, and the barman had grinned at Collins but evidently thought she needed to catch up on her sleep before the next boatful of camera-happy tourists pulled up on shore. The barman dried glasses behind the bar, watching an African Nations League football match on a wall-mounted television with the sound muted. The bar was open-ended with the lake shore at one end and the gravelled carpark at the other. There was a fenced-off area for swimming on the beach, with three sides of wire barriers to deter crocodiles, but it wasn't the safest looking because any crocodile with the inclination to wander around the fence on the beach could simply lie in wait. Collins sipped some more of his beer and looked up as a white taxi drove across the loose gravel and parked in front of the bar. The man got out of the rear, paid the driver and had obviously paid for him to wait, because the driver lowered his seat and closed his eyes and took the opportunity for forty winks while his fare stopped for a drink.

Collins regarded the man with a curious mix of affection and disdain, much like one did a strict parent or guardian. There was much to be thankful for, and much to resent. After he had killed his own bed-ridden mother, rotting from cancer and in agony with every laboured breath, Collins had migrated south from Zimbabwe to South Africa where he lived on the streets of Pretoria and Johannesburg before venturing to the coast, ending up in East London and then Durban. At the age of sixteen, he had met the man now ambling towards him, and that man had changed his life. Preet Du Plessis was a former police officer-turned-mercenary who had plied his deadly trade all over the African continent. Collins had first worked for him as a runner. Du Plessis was involved in every illicit activity from drug-running and prostitution to contract killing. Collins had been tough and impressionable and had killed for money for the first time at the age of seventeen. He had walked up to the police inspector as the man had fumbled for his keys on the doorstep to his home and emptied the five-shot cylinder of a .38 revolver into the man's head. A year later, and he was working as a mercenary in the Congo with Preet Du Plessis calling the shots from the safety of his beachside Durban home. Du Plessis had seen something in Collins – perhaps it took a killer to know a killer – but he had been killing ever since. In some ways, he despised the man for it, and in other ways, he was grateful for the work, the money and the life he had made for himself. It was only when Preet Du Plessis had gone to prison for four years for his involvement in gun running that Richard Collins had crossed paths with Peter Stewart and been recruited into MI6.

Stewart had played a pivotal role in shaping Collins's life, taking a raw, unrefined individual and moulding him into something far more sophisticated and effective—a true work of art. Under Stewart's guidance, and within the clandestine confines of his department at MI6, Collins found a renewed sense of purpose. The organisation provided not only a structured environment but also the opportunity to continue the kind of work that, despite its risks and moral ambiguities, he was drawn to and excelled at. Yet, this new world came with its own set of rules. Though these regulations were sometimes interpreted loosely, they remained a constant presence. Over time, Collins began to feel their weight pressing down on him, the restrictions growing ever tighter—almost suffocating. It was in this state of mounting frustration that he saw Preet Du Plessis again for the first time in six years. The sight of his old mentor, grinning broadly as he approached, brought Collins an unexpected sense of relief, as though a constricting coil had finally loosened around his neck.

# Chapter Fourteen
## Uganda

To gain an unobstructed view of the military base, King had carefully constructed a concealed hide that blended seamlessly with the surrounding landscape. He worked with meticulous attention to detail, ensuring that every element of his makeshift shelter matched the terrain's unique features. The hillsides of West Uganda, much to King's surprise, bore a striking resemblance to the Scottish Highlands. The contours and vegetation of the region evoked vivid memories of his time spent training with Stewart on the rugged Scottish peaks. The altitude here contributed to markedly cooler conditions, with temperatures at least 10°C lower than those found at lake level in the capital. As King settled into his hide, the brisk air and familiar scenery reminded him of the particularly hot summer sessions he endured during his training, reinforcing both his sense of preparedness and his ability to adapt to demanding environments.

King had used the natural cover. He had cut bushes and tied them together and with great attention to detail using paracord. He made sure not to have the underside of the leaves showing, and that the bushes were the right way up. He had then crested the hill on his stomach, moving like a sniper with his elbows and toes propelling him along, unrushed and always hidden behind the collection of bushes. When he had found the most advantageous spot, he used some pegs that he had whittled to hold the bushes firmly to the ground and trimmed more foliage to thicken the areas around him. Barely pausing for breath, King scraped the ground until he had cleared it down to the bare earth, then dug further to form a channel slightly deeper than his prone body, so that he was below the surface and quite out of view from every direction. With the camera and binoculars resting steady on the pile of earth, he could now keep his movements to a minimum as he surveyed the base below. It was a curious decision to site a military base in the low ground. Tactically it would be prone to attack, but King supposed that regular patrols and forward operating bases closer to the border with the Democratic Republic of Congo would act as an early warning system. King had known of a few bases in Afghanistan that had been built in this manner, and they had all come close to being overrun by the Taliban at some time or other.

King could see the reasoning, though. There was a decent road running beneath the base, and such tarmacked roads were a rarity in this part of the region. The presence of reliable road access would have been a significant factor in the decision to site the base here, as movement and supply lines could be maintained far more effectively. In addition, a small lake, fed by rainfall and runoff from the surrounding mountains, provided the base with an unlimited water supply. This natural resource ensured that the garrison would not struggle for fresh water, which was a crucial consideration for any long-term military presence in such remote terrain.

King studied the base and made notes in the notebook in his shorthand. Three barracks blocks, a cookhouse and an admin block were easily identified by the comings and goings of personnel. A fuel dump was located at the far end of the compound away from other structures and the motor pool was located at the opposite end because nobody wanted a vehicle fire near the fuel depot. King supposed that one of the buildings was a shower block, but there was no way to confirm because the troops were embarking of patrols or training exercises. The base had three points of security that needed addressing if they were to achieve their objective. The entrance was manned by a sangar of sandbags, behind which, two men manned a twin .50 calibre machine gun fixed to a swivel mount. That was bad news in a box that they were not going to risk opening. The next issue was the two guard towers placed at each end of the base. The towers were thirty feet high, supported by four wooden telegraph poles for legs and fitted with tin roofs. King could see some type of GPMG mounted in each tower, but from this distance, wasn't sure which type. Not that it mattered, anyway. They would be full powered 7.62 mm or a ballistic equivalent and would rattle off belt-fed ammunition at around eight hundred rounds per minute. That was thirteen bullets per second with a range of over a thousand metres. Another couple of reasons why getting this right was so important.

In the very centre of the base, a cottage stood out in sharp contrast to its stark military surroundings. The building was framed by a neatly maintained garden and enclosed by a pristine white picket fence. The effect was almost comical—surreal even—but there was no mistaking its reality. General Mantutsi, who was widely thought of as being more than a little mad, had chosen this peculiar residence, and his decision seemed to reinforce his reputation. To King, the cottage looked rather like something out of Disneyland's interpretation of an English country cottage. There was no sense of age or authenticity to it, and several details appeared entirely out of place. What really caught King's eye was the picket fence itself, which seemed more reminiscent of 1950s Americana than anything typically English.

After King had been watching and recording for four hours, General Mantutsi finally made an appearance. The door of the cottage swung open, and the general strode out onto the neatly trimmed grass, pausing just outside the white picket fence. He stood with his hands planted firmly on his hips, his posture brimming with self-importance. The man had intense eyes, almost black, and the scar that ran down the whole right side of his face looked as clear as it had done in the photograph back in London. Chin thrust forward, Mantutsi surveyed the military base as though he were a monarch inspecting his realm, exuding an air of arrogance and absolute authority. King, observing through his binoculars, noted the general's theatrical manner, the way he seemed to command the entire scene by sheer force of personality. The long wait had not been in vain; King's patience was rewarded with a clear sighting of the man who held sway over the entire compound.

King silently assessed the situation. The distance to his target was roughly eight hundred and fifty metres, perhaps give or take twenty-five. It was certainly a challenging shot even for a skilled marksman, but with the advantage of elevation, he considered it possible. However, the real issue was not the marksmanship required, but the problem of

## Crossfire

exfiltration once the task was complete. Suddenly, King became aware of a deep reverberation echoing through the landscape, signalling the approach of a helicopter which then hovered directly overhead. He froze, maintaining a death grip on the bundle of bushes in front of him, determined not to betray his position. Relief washed over him as the aircraft dipped and descended towards the military base below.

King observed the Russian Mil Mi-24 helicopter as it hovered above the base, its movements reminiscent of a dragonfly skimming over lakeside reeds on a sweltering summer's day. The helicopter was formidable, bristling with weaponry—missiles, rocket pods and a 20mm gatling gun mounted beneath its nose. King watched intently as the aircraft landed behind the cottage, on a hidden helicopter landing pad.

In the presence of the helicopter, the previously daunting obstacles—the guard towers, the sangar at the entrance, and even the twin .50 calibre machine gun—seemed to diminish in significance. The odds of successfully assassinating General Mantutsi and escaping alive had now risen to a level that would deter even the most reckless gambler.

## Chapter Fifteen
### Kenya

Stewart had measured, marked, remeasured and double checked. The marks had to be meticulous. He had then used a set of clamps to drill the four small holes into the metal. He then changed the drill bit and carefully, methodically drilled out the threads. Stewart had learned aspects of gunsmithing and was competent in making alterations to aid his craft. He could turn many semi-automatic weapons into fully-automatic; he could make suppressors - or silencers - out of tubing and baffle plates, and he had often shortened barrels and stocks for concealment. He applied the double-sided tape to the picatinny rail, then removed the backing side of the tape and placed the screws into the predrilled holes before carefully lining them up with the freshly drilled holes in the top of the receiver. Once the screws were seated, he screwed them in, pressed the picatinny rail tightly against the receiver and tightened the screws until there was no give. He had earlier removed the ghost ring rear site and foresight post, and with the rail now fitted, he attached the riflescope, then checked the weapon for balance and feel.

## Crossfire

Stewart was working with the FN FAL, a semi-automatic rifle that fired the powerful 7.62x51mm round. This rifle possessed the capability to accurately engage targets at distances up to one thousand metres, provided it was operated by a skilled marksman. Recognising the importance of precision for his task, Stewart had chosen a Schmidt and Bender 5-25 x 50mm scope to attach to the rifle—a high-quality sniper scope typically reserved for bolt-action weapons. Although this particular scope was not designed for use on a semi-automatic platform as it was not a precision rifle, Stewart understood the need to make do with the equipment available, adapting to the situation rather than relying on ideal circumstances. That was the essence of what Stewart and his department did – adapt, improvise and overcome.

Stewart loaded the twenty-round magazine with standard NATO ammunition. He would have preferred some green tip, perhaps Swedish made, but in Africa luxury was scarcely an option. The ammunition was in good condition without any tarnishing and that was the best that he could hope for. As usual, Stewart started out zeroing the scope at one hundred metres just to get some holes in the paper. He was way off centre, the bullets going high and right. He had selected the newest looking rifle and inspected the bore with a pen torch for wear to the rifling or marks from poor quality ammunition and concluded that the rifle had never been fired. He had then checked it thoroughly for movement as he had flexed and shaken it. The weapon was solid, and that reflected in the tight group he had just fired. Grouping was everything. It didn't matter how off-target the bullets were from the bullseye, just as long as they were tight together. He could now fine tune the turrets and bring the next group closer. He fired groups of three shots, only ever adjusting when he had a tight group as this would count for marksman error. By the time he reloaded the magazine he had holes on the squash ball sized bullseye. Next, Stewart aimed at the two hundred metre target and repeated the process. He then set about the five hundred metre target with its fist-sized bullseye and used a pair of binoculars with a higher degree of magnification to assess his marksmanship. With the rifle comfortably putting holes in the ink at five hundred metres, he returned to the one hundred metre target and naturally found the bullets going high. He used markers on the vertical cross in the view of the optic to compensate, always aiming lower and found the bullets close to the bullseye. He alternated between the one hundred and five hundred metre targets until he had the aim points consistent. Stewart then turned to the one thousand metre target, with its bullseye the size of a football. He calculated from memory, taking into consideration the wind strength and the air temperature, and when he had steadied his breath, he fired. He now had to aim higher. From the initial one hundred metre zero, his aim point would be close to five feet above the bullseye, but that was more like three feet as he had zeroed minutely at five hundred metres. Bullets travelled in an arc, and getting distance was all about controlling the arc with point-of-aim.

Stewart allowed the rifle barrel to cool as he reloaded the magazine. He could hear the men shouting – communicating instructions - and using small arms as they went through the last drills for the day, and the training phase. They were fired up and ready to earn the remainder of their fee. Stewart had not heard from King, but that was to be expected. The man was operating alone and there was no playbook for how that would go. He just hoped that King could keep his eyes off Ginnie and concentrate on the task at hand. Hopefully the woman would be on the plane home by now, having given King a good cover passing through immigration and customs. Stewart had often *coupled-up* his agents and the girls in admin would leap at the chance of a few nights away all expenses paid, while adding a sense of duty and accomplishment to what was largely dull nine to five office work, no different to working in any large company. No, King and Ginnie were not the problem. But Richard Collins should have been here by now. The weapons and ammunition had been sent, and the pilot had been paid. Collins should have been on the plane last night.

When the plane failed to arrive that morning, Stewart's instincts began to trouble him. After two decades in this profession, he had learned to trust such uneasy feelings, as they were rarely wrong. All day, Stewart found himself repeatedly glancing at his watch, each check a reminder of the precious daylight slipping away. The situation grew increasingly tense as dusk approached. The pilot had been clear: he would not risk flying into Uganda after dark. To avoid radar detection, the aircraft would need to remain below two hundred feet, a feat impossible to attempt safely at night. In much of Africa, once the sun had set, the darkness was absolute.

Stewart forced himself to let go of the worry, knowing there was nothing he could do about a situation that was beyond his control. He redirected his attention to the task at hand, focusing on the target set against the dimming evening light, precisely one thousand metres away. Carefully, he pressed the wooden stock of the rifle firmly into his shoulder, ensuring a solid and steady firing position. He positioned his eye about an inch from the scope, close enough for a clear view, but far enough to avoid the dreaded 'scope bite'. Stewart was all too aware of the danger: he had witnessed inexperienced shooters come perilously close to serious injury, the recoil of a powerful rifle driving the scope back into an unprepared eye socket with enough force to cause real damage. With practised caution, Stewart settled into position, fully prepared for the shot. He fired, adjusting his aim for the recoil after each shot until he had five shots on the paper. Through the binoculars he could see that three of the bullets had struck the black ink, and two were half an inch outside. He doubted that he would get a better result with such a basic rifle, so he packed up his kit and returned to the cookhouse where the men had now gathered and were hanging a skinned baboon over the grill. Stewart was by no means squeamish, but the skinned beast looked like the lads were trying to cook an eight-year-old boy, and even Paddy's spam, rice and beans creation was suddenly somewhat more appealing. The humour was good, though. The men were all laughing and shouting insults at Chris, who was evidently in charge of dinner. They looked a good team, and Stewart was eager for King and Collins to join them and complete their objective, although the uneasy feeling that he had seen the last of Collins would not leave him.

## Chapter Sixteen
### Kampala, Uganda

King had changed into clean clothes before riding back in David's taxi. He was still filthy, but at least he wouldn't get strange looks as he crossed the reception and foyer to get to his room. He checked his watch, unsure how he felt about Ginnie leaving. By now, she should be airside and well on her way back to London. He had enjoyed his time with her and had never expected their relationship to go beyond professional. She had been part of his cover because young men of fighting age in peak physical condition were often caught up in Africa's problems and causes, but a young couple travelling or undertaking aid work was a different matter.

He trudged wearily up the stairs and paused outside his hotel room, the key held loosely in his hand. Fatigue pressed down on him, and all he truly wanted was the simple comfort of a hot shower, a decent meal shared with Ginnie, and the quiet solace of another night in her company. Yet, he knew those moments were already behind him. Whatever they had shared was pleasant, but it was fleeting— never meant to last, never truly real. With a resigned sigh, he decided there was little sense in dwelling on what could not be reclaimed. Instead, he would simply order a few sandwiches from room service and get an early night, gathering himself before he reported back to Stewart in the morning.

King turned the key, swung the door wide, and immediately spotted Ginnie's pull-along bag resting on the luggage rack next to the wardrobe. The sight brightened his spirits, filling him with anticipation for some welcome companionship. She hadn't taken the flight. They had another night together. The prospect warmed him, and he closed the door behind him and walked into the room.

The sight stopped him in his tracks. Ginnie's lifeless body lying on the bed. She was naked, spread eagled with her wrists and ankles fastened to the bedsteads with shoelaces and two belts. One new of brown leather, the other worn, grey canvas. King recognised the belts as his own, and a glance towards his own open bag on the second luggage rack confirmed that the laces were his also. A pair of trainers lay discarded on the floor, the laces removed. King shuddered as he cast his eyes over her, trying not to pause on her intimate areas. She had been strangled with one of her own bras, and her eyes still bore a look of surprise. He stalked off into the bathroom and returned with a towel and covered her up.

He needed to think. What the hell was the play? Call the police? Call Stewart's satellite phone? Call the embassy and hope to appeal to the resident spook? He imagined the consulate would hang up on him and pull down the shutters. No, this was going to be his mess, and his alone to clear up.

King took out his knife to cut the laces, but the sound of police sirens stopped him in his tracks. He walked to the window and saw three police vehicles heading up the driveway with blue and red lights flashing and their sirens now echoing off the building. Behind them, a pick-up truck full of soldiers wearing military fatigues and carrying rifles braked suddenly and the men spilled out the back and over the sides. King grabbed his passport, took one last look at Ginnie, then charged out of the room and down the corridor.

He could hear a commotion downstairs in the reception and foyer, shouts and the sound of heavy boots on marble. He reached the end of the corridor and kicked open the fire escape door. Two police officers were on the lower flight and looked up as he stepped out onto the steel mesh staircase. There were shouts in English, though almost too heavily accented to hear every word. King climbed the fire escape two stairs at a time, his heart racing as he heard the footsteps behind him, and when he heard the gunshots, he ducked his head instinctively, although the bullets sparked near his feet as they struck the grating. He reached the topflight and practically threw himself around the fire escape walkway. Ahead of him, a dead end loomed with just a waist-high bamboo railing, and twenty-feet below, the grass roof of the poolside Tikki bar. King didn't pause a beat as he caught the bar with just his left hand and vaulted over the side. His stomach and internal organs felt as if they were failing to catch up with the rest of him, as the sensation of falling a long way so often felt, and he found himself instinctively holding his breath as he sailed through the air. He impacted heavily, but the roof cushioned his fall, and he broke through the grass thatching and landed between two tables. There were shrieks and shouts from the unsuspecting group of people sitting at the table with drinks, dried grass, wood and debris showering them and in the chaos a table was knocked over, adding broken glass into the mix. King shook himself off, then ducked down as the police officers opened fire from above. A woman wearing a tight-fitting white dress was caught in the volley, crimson spreading quickly across her chest. Another innocent bystander was hit, this time a large American man wearing a Hawaiian shirt who hobbled for safety clutching his leg.

King could not assist either of them, but his training had already assessed the man to be a low-attention priority casualty, and the woman to be past assistance as the dress was now almost completely red and the blood was already pooling on the hard, wooden floor. King did not have time to think about the carnage behind him. He just needed to escape. He charged out of the bar and across the patio, leaping clean over a low barrier of cactus and onto the lawn. A police officer and a soldier stood ten metres in front of him, both holding two-way radios and listening to an array of panicked monologue. They did not seem to comprehend that their suspect was sprinting towards them until it was too late. King drove a powerful front kick into the soldier's stomach, but his momentum not only sent the man sprawling backwards but took King off his feet. He managed to grab the police officer and pull him to the ground with him, then rolled until he was on top, and drove a fist down into the man's face several times until he was out cold. The soldier was on his knees, vomiting. He realised that he did not have the luxury of time and started towards King, but King had already pulled the Browning 9mm pistol from the police officer's belt holster and he pistol-whipped the soldier mercilessly, blood, teeth and spittle spewing over the grass. King got to his feet and tucked the pistol into his waistband before picking up the soldier's Uzi 9mm machine pistol. It was an old model with the open bolt and breech design, meaning that the cartridge was clearly visible in the top of the magazine. Pulling the trigger would drop the bolt, chamber and fire the round, instantly ejecting and repeating the process for as long as King's finger remained on the trigger. The plus points of this was that the weapon was easy to use and know if it was loaded, but the system could be susceptible to debris getting into the working parts. King inspected the chamber in the dull light from the garden lights as he ran to the hotel entrance.

King saw both vehicles ahead of him with nobody standing guard, no drivers behind the steering wheels. He sprinted hard. Police, crime agencies and military all had different ways of doing something, but standard practice was leaving the keys in a vehicle. Nobody wanted the driver to go down with the keys in his pocket leaving the rest of the team unable to pursue a suspect. Even so, he hoped and prayed as he ran that his luck would hold out, and the Ugandan security forces thought the same.

They did. King chose the pickup truck, because as far as he could see, it was a regular vehicle and not liveried as the two police vehicles were. He started it, turned it around not caring for the hotel's lawn and garden edging, then slammed the brakes hard, and slotted the gearbox into neutral. King stepped out of the truck and walked calmly to the front of the first police vehicle. He shot out both front tyres and put a dozen rounds through the front grille into the radiator, fan and engine block. He did the same to the other vehicle and tossed the Uzi onto the ground beside it. Both vehicles steamed from their hot engines, and fluids gushed out onto the ground. He accelerated down the drive, the tarmac new and unworn. The hotel had only recently been constructed and the gardens looked so immaculate and newly landscaped. King pulled out the pistol and readied himself for the roadblock, but in their haste the police and army had not thought further ahead than making a hard arrest. The truck slewed out onto the rutted and potholed road and King pressed on hard, overtaking slower moving vehicles and not pausing for people crossing the road, forcing them to throw themselves out of the way.

After a couple of miles, King took a series of turnings, putting obstructions and distance between himself and the hotel. He slowed down, paid more attention to his mirrors, and tried to come up with a plan. What had just transpired was a classic set-up. Ginnie had been sacrificed and used as bait, and King had been the prey. But who would have done this? His mind kept flashing back to Ginnie's naked body, the look upon her face, the vulnerability of her nakedness. He had enjoyed her body, as she had his own, but there was something sadistically raw about her nakedness. It was more than her death. She had been killed, and that was that. But who had her naked body been so mercilessly posed for. Her breasts, her genitalia – all laid bare for the purpose to shock. Somebody had not only intended to trap King, but to hurt him, too.

King pressed on, his thoughts taunting him. He had no enemies here. He had conducted two reconnaissance operations, and he had gotten away clean. The two soldiers had been an unfortunate incident, but he had disposed of their bodies and gotten clean away. If the bodies were discovered, then it would be obvious to all that they had simply wandered too close to the river and the crocodiles along the riverbank. Hundreds of people on the African continent died every year from crocodile attacks. He was sure it was something like a thousand deaths a year, compared to around five a year worldwide from sharks. It happened.

As King reflected upon the scene, he grew increasingly

certain that Ginnie had not been sexually assaulted. There were no signs that she had been targeted by a group or an individual driven by sexual motives. The very thought of such a possibility filled him with revulsion. Instead, as he examined the circumstances and considered all the details, it became clear to him that the way her body had been arranged was deliberate and calculated, done after she had died. Which meant that King had been the intended victim, here. Somebody wanted to hurt him, and as fantastical as it sounded echoing around his head, it still did not make sense.

# Chapter Seventeen
## Southwest Uganda

The mountains of southwest Uganda are renowned for their striking natural beauty and unique ecosystems. This region is celebrated for its national parks, where dense, impenetrable forests blanket the mist-shrouded peaks. Within these forests, a remarkable diversity of wildlife flourishes, most notably the elusive mountain gorillas that make their homes high among the hills, carefully avoiding contact with humans.

The hillsides themselves are a vivid green; their lushness owed to the area's substantial rainfall and the cooler climate that distinguishes the mountains from the surrounding flatlands and savanna. The persistent mist and frequent precipitation create an environment where vegetation thrives, resulting in a landscape that appears almost otherworldly in its richness and vibrancy. It was a place where despite the presence of park rangers protecting the gorillas from poachers, a person could hide. There were many people hiding in the landscape. Some were criminals wanted by the Ugandan authorities, but the men in front of Preet Du Plessis and Richard Collins were all members of the Rwandan Patriotic Front (RPF), a rebel group composed mostly of Tutsi exiles, who launched an invasion into Rwanda from Uganda in 1990, and again in 1994.

Motu Manasi stood before them, an imposing figure towering at six foot four. Collins, observing him closely, estimated that he weighed somewhere in the region of seventeen stone. The mist that settled in the air clung to his skin, making it glisten with moisture. His complexion was as black as coal, yet possessed the smoothness of satin, a striking contrast in the subdued light of the mountains. Manasi's attire was minimal but purposeful: he wore only a bulletproof vest and a pair of combat trousers. His bare arms, exposed to the cool mountain air, were heavily muscled and bore the marks of past battles—scars crisscrossing the surface in silent testimony to his experience and resilience. Either side of him, two tough-looking men watched them, but said nothing. One of the men was young and fit, the other a decade and a half older than Motu Manasi, and he had the look of somebody high up the chain of command.

"I am paying you a great deal of money, Mr Du Plessis..." Manasi said pointedly, almost accusingly.

"And you will get the result you desire," the South African replied measuredly.

"If you think that you can take my money and run..."

"Mr Manasi..." Preet Du Plessis interjected. "With respect, you have launched attacks and incursions and each time you have been beaten back over the border because you are a band of rebels... brave... but a band of rebels all the same. What we can give you is unity. When we strike, we do so with precision and upon someone with great importance, who you would never otherwise be able to get to."

"You underestimate us, *muzungu*..."

Du Plessis smiled at the racial slur towards a white man. "I will not get into a name calling competition with you, Mr Manasi." He paused. "However, your fee guarantees your cause success. Because we will achieve your objective."

Manasi regarded the South African for a moment, then turned his stare to Collins. "And you're the man for this, are you?"

"I am."

"You don't look much."

"Looks can be deceptive," Collins replied coldly.

"I could test you," Manasi persisted.

"You could," Collins replied tiresomely. "But your payment and me achieving your objective should be test enough."

"Do you enjoy a fight?" asked Manasi.

"No. I enjoy winning."

"I have a man who is the best fighter we have," the Rwandan grinned. "If he beats you, then how about you take a hundred thousand dollars off your fee?"

Collins did not reply, but he looked at Du Plessis, who smiled back at Manasi. "We don't generally go in for games, Mr Manasi. However, we could all use some entertainment. But it goes both ways."

"What do you mean?"

"Let's up the odds."

"To what?"

Du Plessis shrugged. "If your man beats my man, then we will do the job for free..." He paused. "But if my man beats your man, then our fee doubles. You just have to work out whether you want to play games or do good business."

Manasi looked at both men with contempt, then smiled. "I am willing to gamble. I have learned that good business is merely a gamble, so I have nothing to lose." He walked across the hut to two large duffle bags and unzipped them. "Each bag contains one million US dollars. One million was your fee. If my man wins, you do it for nothing. If your man wins, then both bags are yours..." He turned to the men beside him and smiled. "What do you think? Gordi will turn this scrawny *muzungu* into chopped meat for Boerewors..." he said of the traditional South African sausage popular in Uganda and Rwanda, where you could always catch the smoky aroma on the air.

"Very well," Du Plessis shrugged.

Manasi smiled, his confidence undiminished, and gestured for the others to follow him outside. As they stepped into the open air, he caught sight of a small boy passing by, clutching a well-worn football under his arm. The boy's shorts and T-shirt hung loosely from his thin frame, the fabric little more than a filthy rag, and his bare feet sank into the ankle-deep mud with each step. Manasi called out to the boy, who looked up at him with wide eyes. After a brief exchange, the boy nodded eagerly and darted away, sprinting across the muddy clearing. He disappeared quickly into one of the several bamboo huts with grass rooves that dotted the area, leaving the group waiting in the heavy, humid air.

"What the fuck have you got me into?" Collins said quietly.

"You'll be okay."

"I know I'll be okay," he replied somewhat arrogantly. "But what are we doing with this joker?"

"A million dollars, bru." Preet Du Plessis paused. "And now it looks more like two million to me..."

The little boy came out of the hut shouting and shrieking, which drew more children out of the other huts and some tents and lean-tos nestling between the back of the huts and the rainforest beyond. Three women shuffled out of the hut, all cradling babies with one of them breast feeding on the go. A man followed, if you could call him a man. He stood close to seven-feet tall and would have weighed at least three times that of Collins' eleven stone.

"Are you sure about that?" Collins said quietly.

Du Plessis stared at the giant, then turned to Collins and said, "I want both of those bags of money, my friend..." He paused. "Doing this job for gratis isn't going to cut it... so do what you do, and don't leave anything to chance."

Collins studied the man as he walked through the mud towards them. It looked like the man favoured his right knee, but most people carrying around thirty stone would be favouring something. He looked at the meat around the man's shoulders. There was a lot of muscle there, but a couple of rolled gammons worth of fat, too. The man wouldn't be able to scratch his own back, so he wouldn't have the flexibility to reach Collins should he manage to get him into a head lock or choke hold. However, the theory of fighting was one thing; making it work was quite another. What he knew though, was he couldn't chance being hit by the man, because if he took a full swing to the jaw or temple, then it would likely kill him. So, if the man was going to bring his wives and children to a fight, then he'd better be prepared to lose face damned quick. There was much at stake here. Preet had gambled their money on nothing more than a man's ego. And then there was the added risk that if they did double their fee, then they may not even get out of here alive. The RPF were a rabble, but they were a rabble of a hundred in this hideout alone. It was estimated that some fifty-thousand fighting aged men were hidden out in Uganda, the Democratic Republic of Congo and Tanzania waiting for the day when they could take back Rwanda.

More people were gathering around, creating a natural ring for the two men to fight inside. Many of the men had rifles hanging from their shoulders on slings and the women seemed to be in a state of semi undress and were either pregnant or surrounded by small children hanging around their legs.

"You'd better not lose," Preet told him, as if he had to reiterate his point.

"From the size of the crowd, I think it will be better for us if I do lose..."

"You don't get these kaffirs, my friend. They need whipping back into their natural place. You show them who's boss, and they'll fall back into line." Preet paused, giving him a wink. "They may all talk about freedom, but they are only ever comfortable being told what to do. Either by white men, or by their dictator brothers. You watch. They'll get their revolution, but they won't know what to do with their freedom and the cycle will continue until the next revolution. That's why it's called *revolution*, because it always *revolves*."

"I couldn't give a fuck about their freedom, bru. I just want to live long enough to spend my share of the money."

"Then don't go down," he replied. "But if you do, don't fucking stay there..."

Collins did not respond. He walked out into the centre of the ring, rolling his shoulders to loosen them as he stared at the giant. The giant kissed all three of his wives, and several children hugged his legs as he strolled into the ring.

Collins thought about his fee and doubling his money – or losing it altogether – but he also thought about the man's sheer size and weight. If he pinned Collins down face down into the mud, then he'd drown for sure because no way would he be able to struggle free of someone tipping the scales at thirty stone.

Preet Du Plessis and his band of mercenaries had provided Collins with a brutal and practical education in the art of survival and combat. Under their tutelage, he had learnt not just how to fight, but how to endure and prevail in the harshest of circumstances. Yet, it was the advanced training he received from Peter Stewart, along with the seasoned instructors from MI6 and the SAS, that truly refined his abilities. Their expertise turned raw aggression and instinct into deadly precision and discipline. Collins had become, by any measure, a consummate killing machine—efficient, unflinching, and lethal. In this respect, he was no different from Stewart or King, both of whom bore the same indelible mark of men shaped by war and clandestine operations.

The giant faced Collins, a confident grin spreading across his broad face as he lunged forward, determined to assert his dominance. Collins reacted with practised agility, immediately rushing in to close the distance. He dropped his left leg as he pivoted, creating the necessary angle for his manoeuvre. With precision, Collins delivered a kick, thrusting the edge of his right foot downwards in an arc aimed just above the man's right kneecap. The cartilage detached and the knee buckled backwards, a hinge forced the wrong way. The man's size was his downfall, simply putting too much weight on the damaged joint. The giant screamed, but it was nothing compared to the shouts from his family. Collins stepped back and looked at Motu

Manasi, but the man stared back at him, his expression impassive.

"It is not finished," said Motu Manasi above the jeers of the crowd.

"He's done," Collins replied. "He's not going anywhere without a walking stick."

"Are you a *puss*? I do not pay men with no guts to fight wars for me..." Manasi shrugged. "Maybe I should pay one of my women to do what I am paying you to do. Maybe I should take you into my home and fuck you on all fours like one of my wives..."

Collins glanced at Preet Du Plessis, catching the sharp glare directed his way and the impatient gesture urging him to press on. Turning his attention back to the giant, Collins observed that the man was now incapacitated by the critically injured leg, the pain evident in his stance and the look of agony upon his face. Despite the obvious discomfort, the giant showed remarkable resilience, refusing to go down and remaining on his feet. Collins walked up on the giant, then when he was four paces from him, he charged forwards and leapt onto the man's outstretched leg using it as a springboard as he jumped and drove his right knee underneath the man's jaw. He landed to the side as the giant fell backwards, poleaxed. The giant's knee had completely folded in on itself, and he was unconscious when the back of his head splashed into the mud. Collins stepped over him and smashed the heel of his boot into the man's face. He looked up at Motu Manasi and locked eyes with him, then smashed his heel down again, and then a dozen more times until there was no face left, the man's blood and brains leeching into the mud to form a rusty coloured ooze. Collins did not stop as the man's children fell beside their father in the mud, clawing at him and begging for the brutality to stop.

He did not stop even as the man's skull gave in and all that was left was the man's lower jaw, and when he finally stopped stamping his military boot into the mess of hair and brains and bone fragments, he kept his eyes locked on Manasi's own and felt a surge of satisfaction when the rebel leader could no longer hold his stare.

# Chapter Eighteen

"Why the hell would Collins do that?" Stewart shook his head. "It can't have been him. Why would he have done that to the poor girl? It just doesn't make sense."

King thought about Ginnie laying lifeless and naked on the bed, he had been unable to think of little else. "The police were waiting for me to return. They intended to catch me in the room with the..." He stopped himself and sighed, trying to regain composure, then said, "*Her* body..."

"That still doesn't explain why Collins would do such a thing!" Stewart raged. Fifty metres away from them beside their makeshift cookhouse, the men looked their way and Stewart caught hold of King roughly by the shoulder and led him away out of their earshot. "It was probably someone working at the hotel. A pretty, young white woman with golden hair and a great figure. All alone in her room. You know what some of these men are like... they dream of shagging a white woman. It's like the Holy Grail or something... A hotel worker got too close, couldn't control himself and then when his blood and ardour cools down, then he's faced with what he's done and killing her seems to be the only way out. This sort of thing happens in Caribbean hotels all the time."

"She didn't look to have been raped," King persisted.

"How do you know? Have you suddenly got a medical degree that I don't know about?"

"Use your loaf, Peter. There would be signs, and apart from being naked, then nothing else seemed suspicious. No marks, no bruising, no swelling and no... well, nothing, like that..."

Stewart shrugged. "Fuck..."

"When was the last time you heard from him?"

"He should have checked in before the weapons arrived," he replied tersely. "And he should have been here yesterday morning. The same pilot who delivered the weapons was to have flown him in at dawn."

They walked silently through the brush, both men trying to make sense of the situation. King had driven out of the capital and stolen a boat, where he crossed Lake Victoria into Tanzania. From there he had chartered a private plane and pilot to take him to the GPS coordinates that Stewart had given him for the camp. It had been easy enough. The Central and Southern African bush was awash with pilots looking to build their hours to gain commercial pilot status and go on to train with international airlines, and these pilots were easily persuaded to take cash and forget to fill in their flight log, because training to fly commercial airliners cost upwards of a hundred thousand pounds and every little helped.

"If he has gone rogue, then they will know that we're coming," King ventured.

"To what end?"

King shrugged. "To take the heat off him. Whatever he's

doing, it won't hurt him if half the Ugandan army are on our tail."

"We don't know what he's planning."

"He plied his trade all over the African continent before you recruited him, so he'll have contacts."

Stewart nodded. "There is one name," he mused. "Preet Du Plessis. A small-time shithead who's into drugs, prostitution, gun running and people trafficking. He made a name for himself in Angola and Congo. Well, his mercenaries made a name for themselves. The wanker was sat safely beside the pool in his villa while his mercenaries murdered and raped their way through conflicts. They were no better and no worse than the rebels, gangs and general scum they were fighting."

"He doesn't sound so small time to me."

Stewart scoffed. "Small time person, big time deals. Sometimes the two cannot be easily separated." He paused, kicking a stone across the sun-baked ground and watching it fly, then bounce, then roll to a stop. "I'll make a call to London on the satellite phone. If this Du Plessis turd is involved, then we'll soon find out…"

# Chapter Nineteen
## Uganda

The journey had been punishing, with the vehicle struggling over a muddy road that seemed endless. Each mile brought bone-jarring discomfort, the uneven surface creating deep puddles testing both patience and endurance. Eventually, the tyres transitioned from the treacherous mud onto a stretch of compressed hardcore. Although this offered some relief, the rough terrain persisted for another sixty miles, every bump reverberating through the chassis and the occupants alike. At long last, the wheels touched tarmac. The sudden smoothness of the ride was almost disorienting, the silence inside the vehicle highlighting the stark contrast to the previous hours of noise and vibration. The comfort of the paved road felt surreal, providing a momentary sense of peace after the relentless journey through the unforgiving landscape.

Collins gripped the steering wheel, focusing intently on that road ahead. In the passenger seat, Preet Du Plessis kept a wary eye on the two duffle bags stuffed with cash lying across the rear seats, their contents barely concealed beneath a layer of dust and grime. The windows were so caked in mud that the outside world seemed little more than a blur, and the windscreen was streaked with smears, the windscreen wipers scraping uselessly as the washers had dried up hours earlier. Conversation between the two men was sparse, the oppressive heat of the plains, and exhaustion from the tension of the day, and of the perilous journey weighing heavily on both, and each mile brought them closer to the task ahead.

"You showed him back there," Preet said eventually. Neither man had addressed what had transpired. Preet Du Plessis had been associated with the worst men imaginable, but there was something about Collins that made the other men pale into insignificance. "These fuckheads are used to the law of the jungle. It's the only thing they understand..."

Collins shrugged. "We did the man a favour," he replied. "He wanted that big fella taken out of the picture. Why else would he risk the life of one of his own?"

Du Plessis smiled. "It was always on the cards," he said. "Although we dealt directly with him, Manasi is one of four tribe elders. The giant known as Gordi was the fourth. The man either side of Manasi during our meeting were the other two. The giant has been making his thoughts on Manasi's leadership well known over the past few months and Manasi wanted him taken out of the picture. He can handle the other two if he has to, but the big fella had a lot of support within the tribe. The second million was for doing his dirty work for him, while he can keep his position within the Rwandan Patriotic Front and justify the funds."

"On a gamble?"

"It's common practice with those Rwandans." Du Plessis shrugged. "The bet was done in front of the other two elders, so Manasi could always say that he was trying to get the job done for free, thus saving the RPF precious funds."

"Cunning bastard…"

"He is."

"Not him," Collins corrected him. "You…"

"Hah! You can be a snake or a mouse in this game, my friend."

"And you're a snake…"

The South African laughed. "You know what you are, don't you?"

"Me? No."

"You are the scorpion, bru."

"A scorpion?"

"You've heard the story of the Frog and the Scorpion?"

"No."

"Ah, well, allow me to enlighten you." Du Plessis grinned. "The story of The Frog and the Scorpion is a fable about a scorpion who asks a frog to carry him across a swollen river that he cannot cross. The frog is hesitant because the scorpion might sting him, but the scorpion argues that it wouldn't, as they would both drown if it did. Midway across the river, the scorpion stings the frog anyway. As they both sink and drown, the dying frog asks why, and the scorpion replies, 'It's just my nature. I'm a scorpion'."

"And I suppose there's a moral in there somewhere…?"

The South African laughed. "The moral, bru, is that a person's true character or nature cannot be changed, even if it goes against their own self-interest. You're a killer, bru. And you don't fight it. You accepted it a long time ago, and God help anybody who underestimates you…"

## Chapter Twenty
### Kenya

"Fuck it!" In a fit of rage, Stewart pulled his arm back to throw the satellite phone, then stopped himself thinking better of it and kicked a rock across the ground instead. "Well, that's a damned coincidence too many," he said, regaining his composure. King had never seen the man lose his temper and was both surprised and more than a little curious. Everything Stewart did was measured. Even when he tore strips off a new recruit it was all to serve a purpose. King had seen him break a man down so that he could build him up again, build him into something special – if special could ever be used to describe a killer. He had done the same with King, but now that King thought about it, he could not swear that Stewart had ever truly managed it with Richard Collins. There was something about the man that had remained unfathomable. King suspected that Collins was in fact a psychopath, but he supposed that was a judgment for a psychologist.

"Du Plessis?" King ventured.

"My contact at the foreign office has confirmed that the

man did indeed take a flight from Cape Town to Tanzania. Collins was in Tanzania, and as big a country as it is, I don't buy that kind of coincidence."

"What the hell is he up to?"

"If I knew that, King, then I wouldn't be so fucking worried..." Stewart snapped gruffly. King shrugged. He knew that he really should learn not to think out loud in Stewart's company. The man had always said that; *if you didn't have anything useful to say, then keep your fool mouth shut...*

"We can't go ahead with the operation."

"Why?" Stewart frowned. "We've got the men, you've done a recce, and we have the weapons."

"The weapons that Collins sent across the border," said King. "If he was always going to do a runner or go rogue, then why the hell would he buy and send the weapons..."

"I don't fucking know...!" Stewart interrupted.

"For Christ's sake, boss! It's a rhetorical fucking question!" King snapped. He stared at Stewart, and for a moment the Scotsman looked like he would take a swing at his protégé, but he visibly relaxed, and King knew why. King had made a few mistakes early in his career, but carrying Stewart on his back to the extraction point when he had succumbed to a gunshot wound had given him some credit. Both men knew that Stewart would have died in the Congo had King not dragged and carried him to the point of exhaustion, and beyond. Collins had no such credit, and King guessed that had always been the problem between them. "Collins killed Ginnie and made sure the cops and army were hot on my tail..."

"It still makes no sense, King, no matter how many times you say it..."

King held up his hand to silence him. He still had the

sight of Ginnie in his mind, and he knew that he could trust his gut instincts with this. He was damned if Stewart was going to deny what King was certain to be true, because it felt like Ginnie's death was being disregarded. "It makes *every* sense. He killed her and he tipped off the hotel and the cops. As soon as I showed up, the hotel manager must have tipped off the police. They would have to have been waiting around the corner. It was personal. It was Collins sending me a goodbye gift. But he didn't expect me to escape." King paused. "He sent the weapons as arranged, before my run in with the cops and the army, because I'd bet everything that I own that he's also tipped off the Ugandans. If we go in, then I guarantee we'll be walking into a trap."

"But to what end?"

"I think Collins has a job that will benefit from our deflection. Perhaps even aid his cause." King paused, looking into the middle distance. He could not shake the image of Ginnie out of his mind, and he doubted that he ever would. "If we go ahead with this, I don't only think we'll be walking into a trap, but I'm certain we'll be unwittingly helping Collins to achieve his goal."

"Bullshit..." Stewart shook his head. "You're over thinking it. Collins didn't kill Ginnie, and he's not setting us up."

"Then explain Preet Du Plessis being in Tanzania."

"Tanzania is a big country, and Du Plessis keeps most of the African continent at war with one another."

"So, why isn't Collins here?"

"Maybe he's just run into some trouble? Maybe the guy's dead? People get robbed and killed every second of the day out here."

"I don't buy it."

"I'm not fucking selling it, lad..."

King shrugged and stalked off towards the makeshift cookhouse where Paddy was tending to the roasting of a small impala that Josh had shot, and that certainly looked more appealing than the skinned baboon. The men were gathered around, prodding the embers and slicing off pieces of meat to stuff into long-life burger buns. Stewart had allowed them some beers, too. King picked up a bottle and cracked off the top using the edge of the grill and the palm of his left hand. The men looked at him, guessing that something was wrong, but not knowing him well enough to venture, and certainly not wishing to alienate Stewart by getting involved. King figured out their reasoning, but he didn't care. He wouldn't have said anything, anyway. He and Stewart were in a stalemate of disagreement, but it had nothing to do with anybody else.

## Chapter Twenty-One
### Bamako, Mali

"How did you get it here?"

"It came from the American base at Manda Bay, Kenya," Preet Du Plessis replied, his eyes fixed on the FIM-92 Stinger Missile Launch System on the ground in front of them. The hand-fired system had been laid out on the camping groundsheet along with three Stinger missiles. "It cost the original buyer half a million US dollars."

"Your fee was a bit low, in that case," Collins stated flatly.

"It only cost me a bullet..."

"Oh..."

"The best of all African currencies," Du Plessis grinned. "Accepted everywhere, and readily available."

"I still think our fee is on the low side," Collins replied.

"American dollars, my friend. Untraceable. You get a mil, and I get a mil, bru. Besides, this contract will be a showpiece for our new venture." The South African paused. "And if I remember correctly, your first kill was for less than a few hundred..."

Collins did not reply, the image of his mother rotting in her bed as fresh in his mind as if it were yesterday. His first kill had been for a whole lot less than a handful of dollars, and yet, for so much more.

"Your government contact will be as good as his word?"

"Yes."

"And what about his fee?"

"He gets more than money, my friend."

"What else is there?"

"Position, power, faith, wealth and ideals." Du Plessis shrugged. "And he gets *all* of the above. No, trust me, he would probably have paid to get what we'll be giving him."

"Then it sounds as though you missed an opportunity."

Preet Du Plessis smiled. "He will come in useful later. I just so happened to record our meeting, so I may have a powerful ally in the future, or a man to blackmail. Either way, he will be a valuable asset." He paused, gesturing to the weapon system in front of them. "Have you used one of these?"

"No. But I have studied the handbook and once practised with a dummy model."

"A *dummy*?" Du Plessis did not hide his annoyance.

"At a quarter of a million pounds a shot, my previous employers didn't throw that kind of money around. They don't tend to have spare aircraft to practice on, either. But the sighting system and laser guidance simulation is an accurate representation."

"You'd better be sure, bru."

"Trust me."

"It doesn't look like I have a choice..."

"I'd worry more about the quality of your intelligence than me using this thing," Collins replied tersely. "It was designed for the US army and marines to use against

Russian aircraft, and those boys don't tend to hit three-figure IQs."

"Don't worry about the intel. It's at cabinet level. But I *do* worry about your colleagues," Du Plessis said pointedly.

"Don't worry about those idiots," Collins replied with a smile. "I've made sure they'll be kept busy…"

# Chapter Twenty-Two

"I'm taking General Mantutsi."

"You'll do as I bloody well say."

King shook his head. "Sorry, boss, but that's the way it is."

Stewart glared at him but was met with the coldest eyes he had ever stared into, and that included his own each day in the mirror. It was something he had noticed as King's missions stacked up. As if each killing took something away from the man, but added something else, too. King simply became increasingly dangerous with every operation. "Why?"

"I don't know these guys," he replied. "And they don't know me, either. If what I suspect is true, then the operation will go all to shit, and I'd rather be alone on an op that's gone tits up, than relying on somebody else."

"None taken..."

"I would sit this one out, boss. They are all experienced soldiers, and they have a clear objective. Hang back in a support role and let them go in and get Moffusa Bentuwi out of there." King paused. "Stay out of this one and live to fight another day."

"And if you run into trouble going after General Mantutsi?"

"Then I'll get out on my own. I wouldn't leave you there, Peter, so I'd prefer to go in alone and not have to worry about anybody else." He shrugged. "And I'm a better sniper than you, so…"

"Cheeky bastard…" Stewart said lightly, but King could tell that the man was deep in thought. He knew that something was wrong, but King also knew that the tough Scotsman would not risk his pride. He would never sit on the sidelines while his men went into hostile territory. "Okay. If you want to play, *I'm alright, Jack*, then so be it…"

"Hardly!" King retorted. "I'm telling you, my friend, to stay out of this one and let the mercenaries take the flack. I'm still going into hostile territory to attempt to assassinate a high-ranking military leader, so out of you and me, I'm the one taking the bloody risk!" He paused. "You would be better served finding Collins and putting a fucking bullet in his head rather than setting a foot into Uganda."

## Chapter Twenty-Three
### Mali

Birds flying high, you know how I feel... Sun in the sky, you know how I feel. Breeze driftin' on by, you know how I feel. It's a new dawn, it's a new day... It's a new life for me, yeah... It's a new dawn, it's a new day... It's a new life for me, ooh... And I'm feeling good...

Nina Simone continued the next verse as Collins sipped his black coffee, the singer's voice and words echoing from the radio's speaker and around his mind as he thought about his own new horizons. The sunrise had slipped above the distant mountains, casting its golden light across the rolling landscape. The verdant hills and valleys of Rwanda were now illuminated in a warm, shimmering glow that seemed to touch every blade of grass and every leaf. Although beautiful sunrises in this part of the world were a daily occurrence, there was something about this particular morning that made the beauty feel almost unreal. The sheer splendour of the scene defied the notion that such a view could ever become commonplace, leaving an impression that lingered long after the first rays of sunlight had broken the horizon. The melody playing on the radio seemed to underscore the significance of the moment, blending seamlessly with his thoughts of leaving MI6 behind. He was on the cusp of entering an entirely new chapter in his life — a chapter where he would be the one making the decisions, setting the stakes, and determining the value of a man's life, and ultimately, the circumstances and time of his death. The song's refrain echoed his sense of liberation, marking the transition from a life dictated by orders to one where he alone would chart his course and bear responsibility for the consequences.

Collins finished his coffee and switched off the radio, cutting off Nina Simone and the building instrumental crescendo before the song's climax. The cottage was sparsely furnished, and Collins had not concerned himself with the details of how Preet Du Plessis had sourced it, and from whom. The man had a thousand contacts throughout the continent and had built his empire of killing and misery to something unrecognisable from the days where Collins had run packages of drugs or money or killed a police detective on his own doorstep. Du Plessis had aspirations of taking his services global and for that he would need two things. The first was an assassin who was highly trained and used to navigating international borders. The second, was a high-profile assassination that he could claim credit for. This morning, Collins would provide the man with both.

Collins had already loaded the Stinger weapon system into the back of the Toyota Landcruiser that Du Plessis had provided him, so he picked up the satellite phone and the bag containing the laptop and headed outside. By now, Du Plessis would be back in Cape Town, but Collins had all he needed and once the South African had given him the final details via both text message and email to be certain, then Collins would be ready to move. He checked his watch for the fifth time that morning, then put the phone and laptop bag on the vehicle's passenger seat then returned to the cottage and picked up the can of petrol from the porch. Du Plessis had been adamant that Collins should bleach everything to remove fingerprints and DNA, but Collins knew how easily a single detail could be missed. Fire was far more efficient, and there was every chance that such a remote property would go unnoticed burning down completely to ash.

Collins moved methodically, pouring petrol over the soft furnishings and curtains, ensuring that the flammable liquid saturated the wooden walls as well. He was thorough, emptying the can until only a third remained, then used the last of it to lay a trail of fuel leading from inside the cottage to the door. As he retreated, he tossed the empty can back into the building, careful not to leave any fingerprints or evidence behind. He lit a single match and tossed it into the trail of fuel, and the flames ignited more violently than any Hollywood special effects team had ever recreated. Collins ran a few paces away and the sound of the ignition and combustion echoed around the trees. The cottage was burning in less than a minute and by the time he got in the Toyota and pulled away, it was wildly ablaze like something akin to the house in *Gone with the Wind*.

# Chapter Twenty-Four
## Bamako, Mali

The Food and Agriculture Organisation (FAO) holds a conference every two years and is a high-level meeting for member countries in Africa to discuss the region's food and agricultural challenges and priorities. It serves as a forum for developing policies, fostering collaboration, and promoting the transformation of African agri-food systems to be more efficient, inclusive, and sustainable. Recent discussions at the past two conferences had focused on achieving the United Nation's Sustainable Development Goals, particularly those related to ending hunger and poverty. The purpose is to align the FAO's work with the specific needs of the region, improve food security, and promote sustainable agriculture. Various topics are discussed and cover a wide range of issues including war, climate change adaptation, food systems transformation, and rural development. The next conference was set to be held in Morocco, but this year it was being held in Mali, and for a nation battling warring factions, terrorist organisations and the threat of civil war, it was quite a coup for the developing nation, and the capital city of Bamako had been flooded with last-minute funding from South Africa, Egypt and Kenya, and was receiving an unprecedented financial boost.

Richard Collins had chosen his spot with great care, ensuring every detail was considered. Situated seven miles southeast of the city, his vantage point lay atop a hill that overlooked the vast sago terraces below. The elevated position provided not only a strategic view but also ensured he remained out of sight from prying eyes in the city where security for the conference had been ramped up, with both police and military units manning road bottlenecks and directing traffic. The approach to the hill had been carefully selected as well. The track was wide enough to accommodate the Toyota, which allowed for easy access and a swift getaway if required. Its surface was firm, composed of rolled rocks that supported the weight of the vehicle and ensured it would not become bogged down or stuck at a critical moment. Every element of his plan reflected Collins's meticulous nature and attention to operational detail. His exfiltration had been thoroughly mapped-out and Preet Du Plessis had arranged for another vehicle to be fuelled and at his disposal ten miles further south. Preet Du Plessis's extensive network of contacts would play a crucial role in the success of his partnership and new business enterprise with Collins. Their collaboration was built upon a foundation of complementary skills and resources, allowing each man to contribute unique strengths to their shared objectives. Du Plessis's connections provided them with access to procure vehicles, safe communication channels, and reliable information, while Collins's meticulous planning and operational expertise would ensure that every detail of their future missions was considered and executed with precision. This synergy meant that they would be able to undertake complex tasks with confidence, knowing that each aspect—from logistics to security—was handled by the person best suited for the job. Together, they formed a team whose effectiveness stemmed directly from the distinct qualities and assets each man brought to the table.

Collins had set up the laptop on the bonnet of the Toyota and used a plug-in dongle to roam for a signal. The service provider was a company called *Ikatel* which was a Senegalese telecommunications company and had recently broken the monopoly of the state owned *Société de Télécommunications du Mali* (SOTELMA). Collins knew that the company had used strategically-placed masts outside the country to build a sound network, and he smiled as he looked at the screen of his Nokia N70 and was rewarded with a five-bar signal, which he rarely got in the UK. Once logged onto the shared email account, he placed his phone beside the laptop and waited for the email and text. Timing was everything, but he had no reason to suspect a delay. He checked his watch and there were still a few minutes to go, so he walked around the vehicle to the boot, opened the tailgate and opened the hard, plastic case housing the FIL-92 Stinger missile launcher. One of the split rear seats had been folded flat to make room for the six-foot-long case. Collins opened the case to reveal three, five-foot-long Stinger missiles, each weighing twenty-two pounds. The launcher itself, which included the electronic laser sighting system, handgrip and shoulder rest, tipped the scales at fifteen pounds. Collins checked his watch again and walked around the vehicle to the bonnet where the phone and laptop rested, waiting for the message and email that would be a death sentence for all three hundred and thirty souls aboard the Boeing 777-200 carrying Rwandan leader, President Kwizari Habimana to Bamako International Airport seven miles from where Collins was now standing.

Timing was everything now. For the Rwandan Patriotic Front to claim the attack, Manasi had to call in responsibility before Flight WB-701 was shot down, but that would spark an alert, and the aircraft could be diverted within minutes, possibly even seconds. However, the FIL-92 Stinger missile had a lead range of three miles and a ceiling of twelve-thousand feet. The approach at seven miles would have the aircraft's altitude at a little under ten-thousand feet, given that a constant three-degree angle of descent was standard flying procedure on approach for airliners.

The text message arrived first.

*11.24am.*

That meant that in exactly four-minutes and twenty-seven seconds Flight WB-701 would be directly overhead. Preet Du Plessis had Collins' GPS coordinates and had paid off someone in air traffic control. Collins checked the laptop, refreshing the emails. The email was there confirming the time. 11.24am. Collins walked back to the rear of the vehicle and loaded the Stinger missile launcher. He checked his watch. Three minutes to go. If all went according to plan, then Manasi would be making three telephone calls and reading out a pre-written statement. First to the English speaking *The New Times,* widely considered to be a state-owned Rwandan newspaper. The second call would be to *Umuseso*, which was published in the Kinyarwanda language, and the only true independent Rwandan newspaper. The third call would be to the news desk of the *BBC World Service*.

Collins shouldered the launcher and switched on the sighting display. The FIM-92 Stinger missile is an advanced, shoulder-fired weapon system specifically engineered to destroy aircraft. It operates utilising a 'fire-and-forget' guidance mechanism that relies on infrared technology to seek and track its intended target. The fundamental process begins when the operator aims the launcher at the target and waits for the missile's seeker to 'lock on' to the heat signature produced by the target's engine. Once the lock is achieved, the operator pulls the trigger, initiating a carefully orchestrated launch sequence. Collins employed the missile's sights alongside the battery coolant unit, which serves to cool the guidance sensors to optimal operating temperature. When the seeker had successfully acquired the heat signature of the target, a tone would sound in Collins' earpiece and would also vibrate against his cheek, signalling that lock-on has been achieved. Collins looked overhead, checking his watch. Ten-thousand feet above his head, the belly of the aircraft was visible, the sunlight glinting off its wings. He checked his watch. Right on time. He gave it a few seconds for the aircraft to pass over him and waited until he estimated that it was two miles clear.

This was it. Collins took a deep breath, and sighted on the rear of the aircraft, now just a glimmering speck in the sky. He got tone, and vibration. Finally, he squeezed the trigger and the missile propelled from the tube in an underwhelming fashion, powered by the small rocket that would send it the first hundred metres. The two-stage solid rocket motor ignited, and the missile tore upwards through the sky quickly reaching Mach 2.54, or approximately 1,930 miles per hour. Collins watched through the view-finder, keeping his finger on the control in case he needed to make minor adjustments to the missile. His heart was racing as he watched the missile snake through the sky, white smoke billowing from its tail. Collins found himself holding his breath. He had intended to count the seconds, but the sight of the missile left him transfixed right up to the moment it flew directly into one of the aircraft's engines and detonated. Collins could not see in detail, but the wing was blown apart and the fuel tanks ignited and half the starboard side of the fuselage had been torn open like a can of sardines, the aircraft instantaneously losing cabin pressure and the ball of burning fuel incinerating everyone and everything inside. There was a secondary explosion as the other fuel tank erupted, and when Collins rested the launcher on the ground and picked up his binoculars, he could see nothing but falling debris glinting in the sunlight, with trails of smoke from super-heated pieces of metal spinning through the air.

Turning his back on the burning debris, Collins picked up his phone and replied to Preet Du Plessis' text message.

*Job done.*

# Chapter Twenty-Five
## Uganda

Two thousand nine hundred miles southeast of the official crash site of Flight WB-701, King had arrived at the designated LUP, or laying up place. His approach was meticulously timed to take advantage of the cover provided by darkness, ensuring he remained undetected. Moving carefully through the night, King selected a position from which he could observe his target without risk of exposure.

Before dawn, King began preparing his hide. He worked methodically, hollowing out earth to create a concealed space and cutting turfs and foliage to blend the LUP seamlessly into the surrounding landscape. This attention to detail allowed him to establish a vantage point that was both secure and discreet. From his concealed location, King had a clear and uninterrupted line of sight to General Mantutsi's residence. His observation post was positioned seven hundred metres away, with a twenty-eight-degree elevation that offered a direct view of Mantutsi's front door. He had chosen a different position from his earlier surveillance, in the event that his previous position had been discovered. The new position was easily reached under the cover of darkness, and closer to the camp for a better chance of an accurate shot.

King rested the rifle on the layer of turfs in front of him, making use of the natural camouflage he had painstakingly prepared in the darkness. The dawn air at this elevation was bitingly cold, with every exhalation threatening to reveal his position. To counter this, King breathed carefully into his sleeve, minimising the visible vapour that could give him away to any watchful eyes in the vicinity. The action of the FN FAL was locked backwards with the magazine disengaged, and he had two 7.62mm rounds warming under his left armpit. The FN FAL wasn't a precision sniper rifle, so he was taking every precaution possible.

As morning broke, the camp gradually stirred from its slumber. Men emerged from their Nissen hut barracks, some lighting cigarettes as they exchanged quiet words or simply lingered in the chilly air. The sentries stationed in the watchtowers were visibly affected by the cold, rubbing their arms briskly and stamping their feet on the wooden boards to restore some warmth. Although the air was still biting, it was only an hour past dawn, and soon the rising sun would bring with it the oppressive heat that would press down on the men as the day wore on.

As the first hints of movement appeared within General Mantutsi's cottage, the lights flickered on, casting a faint glow through the thin curtains. King, alert to every change, retrieved the two bullets he had been warming beneath his armpit and methodically loaded them into the magazine. With calm precision, he readied the weapon, ensuring each step was deliberate and silent. The barrel of the rifle felt icy beneath his fingers, its chill a stark reminder of the dawn's lingering cold. King spat into his hand and rubbed it briskly along the metal, attempting to dispel the numbing cold that threatened his aim. Cold barrels meant a poor shot, and it was ironic for a sniper, who by their very nature relied upon the element of surprise and to remain unseen, that the second shot was always more accurate than the first from a cold barrel. Once satisfied that he had done all he could, he settled back behind his makeshift cover and raised the rifle, bringing the crosshairs into sharp alignment with the cottage door. He steadied his breathing, preparing himself for the moment when the door would open and the target would emerge into his line of sight. All that remained was to wait.

King had re-zeroed the rifle back at the camp in Kenya, only needing to make a few minor adjustments to suit his shooting style. Stewart had procured a Nissan Patrol SUV and together with the aid of Josh who had served in the Royal Engineers, they had disconnected one of the vehicle's exhausts and routed the manifold through the other exhaust pipe, then cut the disconnected pipe lengthways and stored the weapon, ammunition and four grenades inside before taping it up with silver duct tape. King had then driven over the border using his cover as a freelance nature photo-journalist, while Stewart and the men would be flown in low in a helicopter piloted by a man on the payroll of a rival government minister who was behind the potential coup. The pilot would then pull back to a pre-arranged extraction point. David, who had picked up King and Ginnie from the airport and taxied King on his reconnaissance missions, would wait at a pre-arranged point as a second resort if they failed to make the helicopter extraction point.

King's heart rate slowed as he accepted the situation. This wasn't just about taking a man's life, and nor was it about making a long-distance shot when it mattered – it was about so much more – because in the valley below there were several hundred men and an attack helicopter. King knew that it would take a miracle to make the shot and get out of the area alive, but he had still found the mission to be a better alternative than going into an area that he felt sure that Collins had already compromised, and with men whom he did not know and had not trained with.

The door to the cottage opened and General Mantutsi stepped out onto the path, scratching his head with his left hand and holding a cup of something hot in his right. He was dressed in a plain white vest and camouflaged combat trousers; his feet clad in flip-flops rather than the regulation army boots. King watched the man with a sense of curiosity, scrutinising every detail. This seemed almost too simple. Was it possible that he had misjudged Collins? Mantutsi's demeanour was far too relaxed; he showed no signs of a man who had been warned about an imminent attempt on his life. Everything about his casual appearance and unguarded behaviour suggested that he was oblivious to the danger lurking nearby. But try as he might, King could not help feeling that something was very different from the man he had earlier observed. The air of arrogance wasn't there. Or if it was, then it did not appear as strong somehow. Was the man aware of the threat? Was he merely taunting death? King adjusted the magnification on the scope, but it was still underpowered compared to his Zeiss binoculars, and he gently laid down the rifle and picked up the binoculars. He locked eyes on Mantutsi, then brought the eyepieces to his eyes, his heart starting to race once more. There was no broad scar. Whoever he was, the man standing outside the general's cottage was not Mantutsi.

He heard the sharp reverberation of the engines and rotor blades echoing through the valley. In that moment, a sudden realisation dawned on King—he had made a critical oversight. So intent had he been on manoeuvring into position to eliminate General Mantutsi that he had failed to notice the absence of the attack helicopter from the camp below. The aircraft was not stationed with the rest of the men as he had expected. Instead, it was approaching from the east, its arrival cleverly masked by the glare of the rising sun. King narrowed his eyes, squinting hard into the blinding light as the relentless thrum of rotor blades grew steadily louder. Despite his efforts, he was unable to make out the helicopter's silhouette against the brilliance of the morning sky. The enemy pilot's tactics were clear: using the sun's position to conceal the approach, turning the attack into a near-suicidal manoeuvre, like a kamikaze, coming in fast and unseen.

King rolled onto his back, the rifle in his hands. There was a breeze coming in from the west and that worked for him. He reached into his jacket pocket and pulled out a smoke grenade, pulled the pin and tossed it down the slope between himself and the approaching helicopter. After four seconds the grenade fizzed for a moment then flashed brilliant white and emitted thick, white smoke which caught the wind and billowed high into the air. He climbed out of his hole and rolled over multiple times to put distance between himself and where the helicopter pilot would be expecting him to be. The heavy thump of a machinegun echoed through the valley, and he felt the ground shudder under the impact of multiple .50 calibre bullets from the aircraft's nose-mounted cannon. King got to his feet and sprinted up the hill, hidden by the smoke. As he reached the top, he turned and dropped onto his stomach, the rifle shouldered and ready to fire. The smoke swirled and he heard a change in engine pitch, and the great behemoth broke through the smoke barrier, its nose raised as it climbed and its belly in full view. King fired. Steady shots, twenty in all, the scope centred on the underside of the fuselage. He rolled onto his back, changed to a new magazine and sprinted down the hillside, cradling the rifle and tossing another smoke grenade behind him. This time, the smoke was orange and the wind was keener blowing up the hillside, driving the smoke to the ridge.

King had eyes on the helicopter. One hundred metres to his right, which put it approaching north to south. King stopped, shouldered the rifle and got off five rounds before two rockets snaked from its weapon pods, smoke filling the air in their wake. King dived onto his belly, sheltering behind a cluster of granite boulders as the rockets impacted near him. One hit the ground before the boulders, shaking the ground and filling the air with heat and noxious smoke, and the other snaked past and detonated harmlessly a hundred metres past him. King's ears were ringing and his eyes stung from the burned solid rocket fuel and smoke, but he could hear the helicopter still approaching, and he pulled the pin on a fragmentation grenade and chanced a look, then released the spoon and threw the grenade high and forwards and ducked back down tucking himself into a ball as he waited. The grenade exploded near the nose of the helicopter, peppering the plexiglass and fuselage with shrapnel and fléchettes. The sudden change in pitch reverberated through him as the aircraft banked dramatically and King picked up the rifle and emptied the remaining fifteen rounds at it but he was back on his feet and sprinting down the hillside without waiting to assess the damage. He changed magazines as he went, but he knew that he had only one remaining after this and was lucky to have survived this long. The helicopter's engine pitch changed

## Crossfire

again, prompting King to risk a look over his shoulder as he sprinted across the uneven terrain. The colossal aircraft loomed into view, bearing down on him with an intimidating presence. Without hesitation, King veered sharply to his left, narrowly escaping a torrent of gunfire that tore through the earth where he had just been. The bullets ripped up clods of dirt and stones, sending debris flying and filling the air with a deafening, thunderous roar. King pressed onward, acutely aware of how close he had come to being cut down, his senses heightened by the near-miss and the relentless pursuit of the helicopter above. Again, he darted back the other way and a short burst of machinegun fire chewed up clods of earth. The pilot would anticipate the move should he do it again, and as the aircraft banked and gained altitude, King stopped and emptied the rifle, bullets sparking against the fuselage and shattering the plexiglass. He changed out the magazines, knowing he only had twenty rounds remaining. This was it. This would be his last stand. He shouldered the rifle and took a knee, his breathing making his aim unsteady. He watched through the scope as the attack helicopter steadied into a hover and he fired, aiming at the base of the rotor blades. A short burst of gunfire was returned and King knew that the pilot was now playing with him. A rocket would do the job – vaporise him into the landscape. King counted off the rounds until he had just one remaining Would he be strong enough to use it? Or would using it be the ultimate act of weakness? Stewart had always said to think carefully about this and not leave the game early. You never knew how it would turn out if you folded your cards too quickly. Know when to *hold 'em* and know when to *fold ' em*.

Almost as if sensing King's indecision, or knowing a beaten man when he saw him, the pilot approached slowly.

Hovering just fifty-feet off the ground, with the nose-mounted machinegun aimed directly at King, the aircraft drew near at a frighteningly steady pace. Invincible and inevitable. And then King saw why. Beside the pilot, General Mantutsi was easily identifiable by the jutting arrogance of his jaw. King could even make out the trace of a scar on the man's cheek. The man was enjoying this, and it left King in no uncertain terms how easily that last bullet could save him from the savagery and barbarism of torture. Central African military leaders, drug lords and rebels were extremely adept at such things. King reached slowly for the fragmentation grenade, at the same time as he turned the rifle over in his hands, clutching the barrel. General Mantutsi smiled sadistically. He had the power. A man sent to kill him was at his end and would blow out his own brains in front of him. King wondered both how and when Collins had tipped him off. Slowly, King thumbed out the ring-pin of the grenade, carefully plotting the distance and height in his head. He doubted that he would ever throw the grenade that far and would likely be cut down before he could make the throw, anyway. He gripped the barrel of the rifle tightly, then unseen behind his back, he released the spoon of the grenade and counted: *one thousand and one... one thousand and two...* Then tossed the grenade slightly in front of him, and stepped into it as a cricket batsman would, finding the scorchingly hot barrel with his free hand and smashing the rifle butt into the grenade with all his might. The impact jolted through his arms from his wrists to elbows like an electric shock, savage enough for him to drop the rifle, but the grenade arced in front of him. *One thousand and three... one thousand and four...* King dived to the ground and covered his ears as the grenade bounced off the cockpit Plexiglas and rose up towards the rotor blades, before detonating and rupturing the rotor struts. The helicopter lurched sideways and flipped over before crashing into the ground upside down, the spinning rotors spiralling in all directions as the aircraft burst into flames.

King stood up then bent down and picked up the rifle. The pilot was clambering out of the wreckage, his legs burning and he writhed on the ground to extinguish the flames. King kept the rifle aimed at him as he drew closer. Mantutsi was struggling to get his harness off, flames licking at his legs. He looked up at King defiantly as King turned his aim to him and fired his last round through the man's forehead.

King dropped the rifle on the ground and turned his attention to the pilot, who was still patting out the flames to his burning trouser legs. King doused the flames with his own water bottle, then bent down and relieved the man of the .38 revolver secured in a shoulder holster, and the man stared up at King with fear in his eyes. King couldn't see over the ridge, but he could imagine soldiers running and clambering up the slope towards the smoke and flames unseen on the other side. He figured the pilot would either tell them where King was headed or he wouldn't. Perhaps he would appreciate the fact that the man they were chasing had doused his legs and decided not to put a .38 bullet through his head. Either way, it was obvious where King would be heading, so he spared the man and simply turned and ran like his life depended on it.

Because it did.

# Chapter Twenty-Six
## Uganda

They moved cautiously through the dense jungle; every step deliberate and measured. Paddy led the way, his experience evident in the way he navigated the tangled undergrowth. Suddenly, he raised his hand, signalling the group to halt. The others immediately froze, listening intently to the sounds of the forest around them.

Stewart, who had carefully studied King's notes prior to their departure, recognised the significance of this spot. According to King's observations, this was the point where the thick jungle abruptly gave way to stretches of agricultural land, the transition as stark and sudden as a monk's bald patch. The team remained on high alert, aware that beyond this natural boundary, they would be exposed and vulnerable. Stewart made his way past the men and stood at Paddy's side and through the thin barrier of foliage, studying the ground ahead of them with his powerful binoculars.

"A click and a half of clear ground, boss," the big Northern Irishman drawled, his accent somewhere between an opera tenor and a tramp gargling with saltwater. "But we can use the edge of the fallow ground like we used to use the hedgerows sneaking up on the boyos in Ulster…"

"Seems doable," Stewart said of the fifteen hundred metres of open ground. "We really need to tuck into that scrubland, though…" If King was right, and there was a possibility that Collins really had tipped them off, then that rough ground could be as full of the enemy as the hedgerows of Normandy had been on D-Day.

"Your man did it."

"Aye, but he's fucking good," Stewart grinned and punched his old friend on the arm.

"Feck off…"

"The water crossing is going to be the problem," Stewart conceded.

"Aye, well, I'll go first and you feckers can race the crocs when they get the message that someone's playing in their pond…"

Stewart signalled for the men to follow. They had all taken up various positions, much like an analogue clock face. Weapons aimed outwards at 9, 12 and 6, while Stewart and Paddy had surveyed the fields at the 12 o'clock position.

Stewart switched the men's positions putting Chris on point. The ex-para and former SAS trooper was a good point man. He was sharp-eyed and was quick to react, and Paddy would need a break from the concentration of being on point. Paddy had been right. The fallow ground had overgrown to form a barrier not unlike a hedge and the men kept close to the reeds, weeds and grasses that had been mixed with various seeds from farming, with corn, maize and sago plants sprouting through the foliage. The men formed a line, twenty metres between each man to cut down the chances of all of them being mown down by automatic gunfire if it all went south. Stewart switched the FN FAL to his left hand, the heavy rifle reminding him, without any sense of nostalgia, of his yomp from Port Stanley to Goose Green during the Falklands War. He had been a young man back then, and the rifle had been a beast to carry on the sixty-mile march. Forced to meet their enemy on foot after their vehicles had ended up on the bottom of the South Atlantic Ocean thanks to Argentine bomber runs, the brave soldiers had battled fatigue, icy winds and sleeting rain, but had taken the fight to their enemy and won convincingly. However, as much as he hated the rifle's size and weight to carry, he would take it every time over the modern, plastic 'pop-gun' offerings used by NATO today. Surprisingly, the FN rifle was around the same weight as the tiny and compact SA80 used by British forces, but it was the sheer length and utilitarian finish of the rifle that made it seem so much more than the sum of its parts.

When they reached the swamp, it was evident that there had been considerable military activity in recent days, judging by the multiple boot treads in the mud. There were many empty bullet cases, too. Stewart could see why after taking just a few steps through the knee-deep water. The remains of several crocodiles lay in the water, or laying across tufts of reeds, their skin peppered with bullet holes. Practically every carnivore in the food chain had feasted on the crocodiles, carrion birds now taking to the wing as they approached and crayfish and freshwater crabs scurrying into the safety of the water. Ahead of them, where the riverbank met the edge of the swamp, several crocodiles basked in the sun, their bellies full. Stewart thought it could either be a blessing that they had eaten their fill, or King had given them a taste for human meat.

## Crossfire

"The army must have found the remains of the two soldiers King killed, and taken it out on the crocs," Stewart mused.

"He must be a fucking machine," Paddy commented. "To carry two bodies a kilometre and a half down here and use the crocs to dispose of them..."

Stewart did not reply. He didn't go in for praise at the best of times and was damned if he would now that King had given him an ultimatum. He just hoped the man would see to killing General Mantutsi without any fuss or comebacks, he would then work out how best to deal with King later.

"We can't risk shooting those fellas," said Chris. "I say we veer off to the left and bypass them, then see what we're looking at upriver."

"Sound," Stewart replied and changed course across the swamp, keeping his eyes on the large crocodiles resting on the riverbank.

They trudged onwards, eyes everywhere, weapons at the ready. When they stepped up onto the sandy bank leaving the swamp behind, the crocodiles downriver had disappeared.

"The fee for this job just went downhill fast," said Josh.

"It's just a swim, pal," Sam replied.

"I didn't sign up for crocs!" Josh snapped.

"You didn't sign up to dig latrines or set up camp, either," said Chris. "What the fuck *did* you sign up for?"

"Soldiering," Josh replied testily.

"For fuck's sake, man!" Paddy shook his head. "This is the last time I vouch for you, pal..."

Stewart ignored the men and stared into the slow-moving water. He slung the rifle over his neck and shoulder and waded into the river without a word. When he reached waist level, he pushed out into the current and swam a steady breaststroke until he could stand and waded into the shallows and up onto the bank. He had always led by example, and now it was for the men to follow his lead. When he looked back at the four men, Paddy was already wading out, and Chris was shouldering his rifle. Stewart unloaded the rifle, worked the bolt a couple of times and shook off the magazine before inserting it again and making the weapon ready. The rifles were well-oiled and could cope with getting wet in the short term.

Stewart made his way up the bank, positioning himself where the dense foliage of the jungle met the open stretch of sand. From this vantage point, he could keep an eye on the others while also remaining partly concealed by the greenery. As he glanced back towards the river, he saw Paddy standing alone on the beach, watchful and steady, keeping a lookout over the water and their surroundings. Meanwhile, Chris and Sam were still in the process of crossing, wading cautiously through the shallows as they made their way towards dry land. The group's movements were measured, each man aware of the need for vigilance in the unfamiliar and potentially dangerous terrain. "Where the fuck is Josh?" he said as Paddy reached him.

The big Northern Irishman frowned and turned around, scanning the river and far bank. "Fuck knows..." He looked at Chris as he reached them. "Where's Josh?" Chris shrugged, quite uninterested, and started to check and dry his weapon, and so Paddy turned to Sam instead. "Where the hell is Josh?"

Sam looked back at the river, then stared at Paddy and Stewart. "He was behind me. I heard him splash as he dived in."

"You saw him dive in?" asked Stewart.

## Crossfire

Sam shrugged. "I figured he dived in, because of the splash..."

Stewart made his way down to the river and scanned the bank and the water, which was dark because of the bottom, but clean enough to see a few feet below the surface. "Fuck..." he said quietly to himself. Could a crocodile have taken him so silently? Nobody else had made a splash as they had taken to the water or waded out onto this side of the river. Stewart walked back up the beach and nodded towards the jungle. "Can't fix what we can't fix," he said. "If we don't see him again, then his fee gets divided among you."

"Fuck, boss," Paddy shook his head. "He may have been a bit of a dick, but he was a great soldier and a good mate..."

"Well, I guess we'll have to take your word for it, man," Chris commented flatly. "But we've got a job to do, so let's get it done..."

"We can't just leave him!" Paddy protested.

"Where the fuck is he, then?" Stewart growled before pointing at the opposite riverbank. "He's not there, and we can see all the way across the swamp to the edge of the fields. He would never have crossed the swamp before we lost sight of him. He's gone. Pure and simple. Snatched by a croc and taken underwater."

"They stash their food," said Chris. "Especially if they've recently fed. They don't miss a kill, simply jam their prey under the bank or into some rocks for later. Softens up the flesh by putrification."

"Putrefaction," Sam corrected him.

"Jesus *fecking* Christ..." Paddy shook his head in exasperation. "The guy was a mate a minute ago and now you're talking like this is a National Geographic documentary..."

"There's nothing we can do," said Stewart and led the

group with calculated caution towards the treeline, sending Paddy ahead to take point. His reasoning was clear—he knew Paddy's capabilities and trusted his judgement. It would also take the man's mind off losing his friend, because nothing focused your mind like being on point in hostile territory. Stewart reasoned that Sam, though highly recommended, remained an unknown quantity in Stewart's mind, and he preferred not to risk the group's safety by relying on someone he hadn't worked with before. Chris, meanwhile, assumed the role of rear guard, his eyes constantly scanning their back trail. He was vigilant, ensuring that no one was tailing them or attempting to manoeuvre them into a trap. The formation reflected Stewart's practical approach to leadership, balancing trust with strategic caution as they moved through the uncertain terrain.

The climb through the jungle was arduous, the incline steep and the way forward choked with thorns, broad fronds, and tangled vines. Each step demanded effort, as the undergrowth clung stubbornly to their legs and packs. The ground beneath them was carpeted in thick, damp leaf litter. Every footfall sent up a fetid stench of decomposing vegetation and decay, a constant reminder of the jungle's relentless cycle of life and death. The air was heavy, muggy, and filled with the sound of insects and distant bird calls.

Stewart had stood Paddy down midway up the slope and now led the way, consulting King's notes to guide their route. He kept their path to the cover of the jungle, deliberately avoiding the exposed, cleared terraces below. Careful navigation was crucial; Stewart's focus never wavered as he steered the group through the dense foliage, determined to reach the summit undetected. Finally, after a punishing ascent, they emerged at a vantage point above their objective: the plantation house and its cluster of surrounding buildings.

"Sam, Paddy, I want you east and west of the plantation house. Chris, you come with me and we'll go in from the south." Stewart paused. "North would have been covered by Josh, but we don't have a choice now. Sam, Paddy, watch your flanks and that'll cover north. There's nothing but steep terraces on the north side, so it's unlikely that they will have that side covered as it would be a bitch of a climb."

"That's a lot to take for granted," Sam replied.

"What fucking choice do we have?" Stewart glared at him. "I didn't bank on losing a man before we even reached the objective. We allow an hour to reach our positions and go in on the hour. Use your knives, if possible, and try not to go noisy early."

"Exfil to the east..." Chris reminded everybody, then repeated the co-ordinates. "We've got a soft exfil flyby in six hours, and a hard exfil in eight. After that, and we're on foot and in the shit."

"If that happens, then four miles due west I have a taxi waiting," said Stewart.

"A bloody taxi?" Paddy frowned.

"A man called David, just off the road near where we came in." He checked his watch, then added, "He'll wait for another ten hours."

"It's a long, fucking yomp," Sam shook his head. "If we get to the chopper exfil and it leaves without us..."

Stewart shrugged. In truth, he had been saving that option for himself. It was how he rolled.

"It's what we've got, and it's what you fucking signed up for, pal," Paddy said gruffly. "Frankly, a back-up exfil sounds like good news to me."

Stewart moved off first, followed by Chris. The slope

down to the plantation was steep and unforgiving underfoot, tree roots and rotten vegetation presenting tripping and slipping hazards, and all the while they checked for snakes coiled on the ground or balanced in the trees. Paddy and Sam broke off for their separate routes and that's when the first gunshot rang out, and all hell broke loose.

# Chapter Twenty-Seven
## ITV News at Ten

"Good evening," the female newsreader looked emphatically into the camera and continued. "We begin tonight with breaking developments in Central Africa, where government officials have confirmed that a commercial airliner carrying the Rwandan president was brought down earlier today under what authorities describe as *hostile fire*. Early reports from military observers suggest that Rwanda Airline's Flight WB-701 was struck by a portable surface-to-air missile on its approach to Bamako airport in Mali. Investigators have not yet independently verified these claims, but government spokespeople say a full inquiry is now under way. Eyewitnesses on the ground reported seeing the missile intercept the aircraft, which was destroyed upon impact. Leaders across the continent have condemned the attack, calling it a grave escalation in an already fragile region. Regional organisations are urging restraint and warning that any retaliatory strike could further destabilise an area already grappling with displacement, food insecurity, and sporadic violence. However, with Motu Manasi, leader of the RPF claiming responsibility in the minutes *before* the attack, it is evident that war has been declared on the Rwandan government. Diplomatic channels are now in overdrive as international partners appeal for calm and press all sides to return to negotiations. Analysts say the loss of the head of state, if confirmed, could reshape the political landscape of the region, with consequences that may reverberate far beyond national borders. We'll bring updates as more verified information becomes available..."

# Chapter Twenty-Eight

"*You're too fucking slow, Lucinda! Bill Neeley dropped the fucking story from war-torn streets in Rwanda and Mark Austin let the world know on the News at Ten, and we haven't even got anybody on the ground yet! And what are you doing? A special report on orphanages in Tanzania!*"

"But, boss..."

"*Get your fucking fanny into Rwanda now and get us a fucking story! Smoke, flames, gunshots and some bodies on the fucking street! The more the better. They like setting tyres on fire around people's necks out there, so make sure you get some footage of that. We'll blur out what's necessary at this end...*"

Lucinda Davenport knew that the producer would have been happy with the orphanage report, had war not broken out in neighbouring Rwanda overnight, and had the channel's direct competition not already been on the ground. Had they had a tip off? Undoubtedly. That fact made her blood boil, because as well as the satellite stations did in the ratings and awards, they were never the first port of call for tip-offs or story inquiries. She cursed Mark Austin with his smug calmness, and Neeley always being the first pair of boots on the ground when war broke out. All she could be thankful for was that Mary Nightingale hadn't been the one to break the story. She had been in the woman's shadow for far too long. Pipped to the post so many times before. The woman looked bloody good in a bikini, too. Lucinda had been offered a guest presenter slot on the travel show *Wish You Were Here*, and then that bloody Nightingale woman suddenly had the gig before her agent could settle negotiations.

"Problem?" Ian Gallagher, her cameraman asked. "Sounds like he's busting your balls..."

Lucinda put her phone in her pocket, not even bothering to pretend that she had not been hung up on. "It was Lawrence, yes. And he was busting my *ovaries*," she replied, then added, "Again." It seemed to be a trait. Having recently made the move from respected print journalist to television news correspondent, she had yet to experience any of the glamour she thought would come with TV work and quietly yearned for the days of filing copy and fluttering her eyes at her male editors when she wanted to run with a thread. She hadn't bargained on her feminine wiles being wasted on her homosexual senior producer.

"What's up? Looks like you voted Labour and got New Labour instead... oh, wait..." Malcolm Selby said as he joined them. He had worked for years at The Guardian and had thought that doubling as Lucinda's soundman and producer would be a good career move, but at fifty-two he was having second thoughts about leaving a comfortable office and his champagne-socialist friends in Notting Hill and Holland Park. His wife and teenaged daughters had thought him mad, but he had explained that at least his midlife crisis didn't involve an expensive sportscar or a mistress, so travel and uncertainty would have to do instead.

"Lawerence," she replied, as if the man's name was all the explanation needed. It was, because Malcolm simply rolled his eyes. "Let me guess. Fuck the orphanage piece, and off we go into a warzone...?"

"Exactly." She checked her slim, gold Patek Philippe watch and said, "Get everything we need to get us into the country as fast as we can." She took out her phone and turned her back on them as she called her husband. Lucinda glanced at her watch again, feeling a fraud. Her heart yearned to write and film the orphanage story, and yet the gift from her husband was a reminder of their extreme, somewhat repulsive wealth. The slim band of gold and complicated movement could build a dozen orphanages and fully fund them for a year. She knew it was madness to wear such a thing amongst such abject poverty but had clean forgotten about it as she had hurriedly packed her bags and raced to the airport. Annoyingly, although entirely predictably, her call was transferred to his private secretary.

"Good morning, Home Secretary's office, Elizabeth Shaw speaking..."

Lucinda groaned inwardly. Despite the seventy-thousand-pound gifts, she had suspected her husband of screwing his secretary for years.

"Hello, Elizabeth, this is Lucinda," she said, hoping to keep the frostiness out of her voice, but knowing that she had failed dismally.

"Lucinda...?"

"The wife..." she said, biting her lip to stop herself saying 'the other woman'.

"Oh... hello Lydia..."

"Lucinda..."

"Sorry, how may I help you?"

"Tell him to ring me," she said curtly. "I need to travel to Rwanda immediately, so tell him to pull whatever strings are necessary..." She hung up, knowing that if her husband was indeed sleeping with his secretary, then the woman had been forewarned. *Damn it!* she thought. The last thing she needed was to tip the couple off that she was onto them.

She cast a glance back at her team, fully aware that not one of them—including herself—had anticipated being assigned to cover the violence of an active war zone. The realisation struck her that, despite their professional backgrounds, they were all thoroughly inexperienced in such circumstances and woefully lacking in adequate preparation for what lay ahead. The unfamiliarity of the situation weighed heavily on her, underscoring the sense of vulnerability shared among them as they faced the daunting prospect of reporting from the heart of conflict. They had no guide, no plan other than to cross over a hostile border, and no contacts on the other side. Malcolm Selby had spent three weeks researching the routes, government agencies, media and broadcasting laws and permissions to film. Lucinda had actively reached out to charities including the Red Cross and Médecins Sans Frontières and gained permission to access the camps and interview their staff and volunteers. They were prepared for an in-depth piece on orphanages and the rising problem – tragedy, even – of the impoverished giving up a child so that they stood a chance to feed their other children. They were not, and would not be, prepared for a warzone.

# Chapter Twenty-Nine

King had given up on trying to get hold of Stewart and sought out David at the airport instead. The local asset was a full-time taxi driver and would be easy enough to find. He had hired a car under one of the aliases that he had been allocated to use and changed up his appearance from what he assumed would still be an APB out on his description. Now wearing a pair of long cargo shorts and a Che Guevara T-shirt and a pair of sandals that he had purchased in a market, King had topped off what he liked to call his 'trust fund wanker' look popular with European travellers all over the world, with a thin woollen beanie made by a popular surf style brand. His small backpack was well-worn and had done almost as many miles as King had.

King had enough miles on the clock and the tan to go with it to look anything but fresh off an airplane and was largely left alone by the locals touting for everything imaginable as he milled around the arrivals of the airport. He bought a cup of terrible tea and waited, then after an hour he saw David and walked right up to him. The man did not hide his confusion, but King could see that he recognised him and said, "I'm hiring you for a couple of days. Let's go…"

King took the lead, leaving David with little room to object or negotiate. His assertiveness made it clear that he was in control of the situation, and David, recognising the inevitability, followed him towards the waiting taxi. When they reached the man's car, King remained true to his word and handed David a wad of cash—an amount he judged to be equivalent to a week's wages for the driver. The gesture was both practical and purposeful, ensuring David's cooperation without further discussion as they prepared to depart.

"I can't get hold of Stewart," he said.

David shrugged into the rearview mirror. "I haven't seen him."

"You took me into the hills the first time," King reminded him. "He was going back there."

"I didn't take him, man…" David shrugged. "He asked me to wait out there for twelve hours, in case he needed a ride, but the time came and went, and I gave the man another hour, then drove home…"

"Have you heard anything?"

"No."

"Take me there now," King ordered him.

"Sure thing…"

King kept silent throughout the hour-long drive, ignoring David's attempts at conversation. The landscape of Uganda passed by his window in flashes, a blur of broken-down buses, passengers labouring over roadside repairs, donkey-drawn carts, and families piled onto motor scooters. These sights, which might fill a traveller's journal with wonder and vivid descriptions, barely registered with King. He had grown accustomed to the everyday realities of the region and took little notice of the chaos and colour unfolding around him. His relationship with Africa was complex. He found himself both drawn to and repelled by the continent, experiencing a mix of loathing and adoration reminiscent of an alcoholic's struggle with drink or an addict's fixation on their next high. Despite everything, there was something in Africa that would forever call him back, even as it pushed him away just as strongly. Something that would continue long after he was ordered there to do MI6's bidding with a bullet.

"Give me six hours," he said as David pulled to the edge of the track. The man had been paid well and did not seem concerned about lazing the day away parked in the shade. "If I'm not back before then, don't wait any longer for me."

King changed beside the vehicle, swapping his shorts for a pair of full-length cargoes and the T-shirt for a long-sleeve shirt that would protect his arms from stinging leaves. He remembered watching the film *Rambo: First Blood Part Two* after completing his jungle survival and infiltration training and laughing as he wondered how many minutes Sylvester Stallone's character would have lasted running around the jungle and crashing through the foliage naked from the waist up. Finally, King swapped the sandals for a pair of desert boots and fastened his knife to his belt and tucked into his pocket the 9mm Browning that he had taken off the police officer at The Emin Pasha Hotel in Kampala and subsequently hidden before fleeing for Kenya.

King trudged into the jungle without a backward glance. His steps were deliberate, betraying none of the uncertainty that might plague a less experienced man. He had already mapped out the route in his mind, each twist and fork ingrained from his previous incursion. The challenges awaiting him were not unknowns; they were familiar adversaries he had long anticipated. King's awareness was acute. The presence of military forces in the area was a given, a fact he accepted with the same grim resignation as one accepts the inevitability of rain during the wet season. Yet, it was the river that occupied his thoughts most keenly. He understood the hazards and the risks that clustered along its banks, recalling every detail he needed to survive what lay ahead. The sight of the crocodiles ripping to shreds the two dead soldiers had been on his mind ever since.

An hour into his trek, King emerged at the edge of the jungle and stopped to assess his surroundings. Before him stretched open fields, their boundaries marked by patches of ground that had once been cleared but now lay neglected and overgrown. In the distance, nearly a kilometre away to his left, he spotted a group of workers toiling in the fields. He considered his route carefully; by skirting along the field's edge where the land was untended and fallow, he reasoned that he would remain undetected. It had worked for him previously, and the workers were occupied with their own tasks and separated from him by both distance and the intervening brush, so were unlikely to spot his movement if he kept to the overgrown boundary.

King was gripped by an intense sense of foreboding as he retraced his steps towards the place that felt, inescapably, like the scene of a crime. The memory of his previous escape lingered in his mind—he had been fortunate to avoid death, capture, or drawing the attention of additional army patrols patrolling the area. Back then, he had managed the situation with precision and had made his escape without a trace. Yet, even as he pressed forward, King was acutely aware that by returning, he was testing his luck once more, pushing the boundaries of fate that had already let him slip through its grasp once before.

## Crossfire

The swamp loomed up on him like a spectre. King could see that there had been activity here. Multiple boot treads in various directions, many different sizes. It indicated that a small troop of soldiers had been here, and it was likely that his ruse with the two bodies had worked. However, through the mess, he was able to pick out different treads heading in one direction. These were expensive civilian boots – not military issue – and he would bet everything he owned that they belonged to Stewart and the four mercenaries. Desert boots like his own pair of Timberlands. Better than military issue in every way. Judging by the impressions of the tracks, and the crust of dried mud around them, he estimated that they were a day old, which would fit right into the timeframe. Stewart and the other men had passed through here.

King used his knife to cut another branch as a depth testing pole, whittling off the small branches and tendrils with the razor-sharp blade. Taking tentative steps into the ooze, he tested and probed the mud and water, his eyes alert and searching for danger. He had thought of little else since the feeding crocodiles had ripped the two dead soldiers apart, and the fear of being back here was tangible.

After twenty minutes, King reached the riverbank. His trek had taken him further south and he was a hundred metres downriver from his previous crossing point, but that wasn't the issue. Crossing difficult ground often took you off course. No, the issue was that what he saw next shook him to the bone. He saw the rifle first, the sling still attached to the body, or more accurately, the head, neck and left shoulder. Everything below the left shoulder was gone, apart from a two-foot length of vertebrae barely held together by flesh and sinew. For a moment, he thought it had been one of the unfortunate soldiers that he had disposed of, forgetting all about skin colour. It was the rifle that first threw him. He had disposed of the two rifles in the swamp and imagined that any search party would have found them partially submersed, held up by reeds and the patches of thicker mud. And then he recognised that the body had belonged to a white man, and his heart had raced further as he thought of Peter Stewart, and the underlying feeling of love he had for the man. He both hated the man, and yet, he realised that he loved him, too. Was this a father-son relationship? He didn't know because he had never had one, but at that moment, he knew how much he owed the man who had rescued him from the cold prospect of a life behind bars and given him a chance for redemption and self-improvement – a purpose that he had never head, never felt possible or remotely achievable. Did a son both love and hate his father? Was that even a thing? He had often listened to men describing their relationships with their fathers, and it had always seemed so complex to King, who had only ever known the fleeting love of various women, and of course, the solid and non-negotiable love of his siblings who were now scattered and uncontactable.

King stepped closer, present in mind enough to watch the water for an ambush from a crocodile, and put the toe of his boot underneath the partial corpse and rolled it over. The crabs, fish or crayfish had been busy, but despite missing an eye and most of his lips – King presumed the creatures had been attracted to the soft parts of their meal – he recognised the corpse as one of Stewart's men. He had not trained with them and so did not really know them, but he could quickly eliminate Chris for his skin colour and Paddy for his mane of brown hair and contrasting red beard and broad facial features. So, it was a toss-up between Josh and Sam. Either way, it was bad news. King unhitched the sling and picked up the rifle. He quickly checked it over and could see that it was fully loaded and made ready. If there had been a fire fight, then the man went down before he could unsling his rifle and return fire, which didn't quite sit right with him. No, King was certain that the man had fallen foul to Africa. If the heat, drinking water, disease and rebel or military factions didn't get you, then the wildlife would.

King looked around him then kicked the remains into the water. The circle of life. It seemed more fitting than to have the man's remains rotting in the sun. A small crocodile on the opposite bank slid down the mud and into the water, and King supposed that was that.

"Rest in peace, soldier..." he said quietly, then trudged up the riverbank to put some distance between himself and a feeding crocodile to make his river crossing in the same place as before.

"Get down, dickhead..." Stewart hissed at him.

King stopped, crouched low in search for the source of the voice.

"Ten o'clock!"

King searched the reeds, then dropped onto his stomach and crawled into them to be met by Stewart's scowling face, bloody, muddy and grimacing in either pain or discomfort, or perhaps both.

"What the fuck...?" King asked quietly.

"We were fucking ambushed!" he replied tersely. "You were bloody right. Collins shafted us, because we went in like fucking ghosts..."

"What happened to the guy down there?"

Stewart frowned. "Josh?"

"I suppose it could be. It's certainly not Paddy or Chris."

Stewart nodded. "That'll be Josh. We lost him in the river crossing on the way over. Nobody heard a goddamned thing..." He paused. "What's left of him?"

"Nothing by now," King replied. "I put him back in the river."

"You're a cold bastard, King..."

"Seemed more fitting than to just leave him there drying out in the sun." King paused. "Are you injured?"

"Just a graze..."

"Let me see."

"Oh, fuck off you soppy bastard. If I say it's just a graze, then it's just a fucking graze..."

"Fuck you, then. Die of sepsis and give me a fucking break once and for all..." King chided. "Where are the others?"

"Sam's dead. Took one right between the eyes, the lucky bastard. Paddy went down, but I saw them dragging him off." He shrugged. "If I fired, then I would have given away my position. God only knows where Chris is, because they were onto him instantly and chased him into the fucking jungle. Too many to fight, that's all I can be sure about."

"Shit..."

"Now that you're here, we can get the fuck out of here."

"You're joking, right?"

"Why would I be joking?"

King shrugged. "Because we still have to get Moffusa Bentuwi out of there." He paused. "I've done my part, General Manasi is dead. With Moffusa Bentuwi free, then Uganda gets a shot at a democracy."

"Fuck Moffusa Bentuwi," Stewart growled. "And fuck Uganda..."

"I know you don't mean that."

"The only honest and good leaders in Africa are the

ones who haven't been bought yet. Look how quickly Mandela succumbed to the corruption of the ANC. And don't get me started on his bloody wife and her advocating burning tyre necklaces as punishment without trial. Bloody gangsters with good PR, that's all they were."

"Maybe it's time for a cardigan and slippers, boss?" King said quietly. "David is waiting six miles to the west off the road. You go and put your feet up, and I'll carry on with the mission and try and free Bentuwi on my own."

"So, help me, King, if I kill one man today, then it might as well be you..." he growled, shaking his head. "Anyway, back up. You killed the general?"

"Yes."

"Well done."

"There is a problem, though. The Rwandan president was killed yesterday. Shot down aboard a passenger airliner with three-hundred-odd people by a Stinger missile."

"How is that a problem?"

"Because the country has fallen into the fastest and most bloody civil war in history, and I'm convinced that it was Richard Collins. It's just too much of a coincidence that Preet Du Plessis was in Tanzania at the same time as he was, and with both General Manasi and the people holding Moffusa Bentuwi aware that we were coming for them, then it sounds like the perfect diversion for Collins. It's the classic cups and ball conjuring trick. Misdirection."

"Fucking hell..." Stewart closed his eyes. "If this is true, then we can expect Collins to tip off the press that British intelligence was behind this, and not only that, then he'll muddy the waters even further and tie us into the Rwanda thing. How many casualties so far?"

"Oh, around a million." King shrugged like it was nothing, but nobody could have foresaw such numbers, on such an unprecedented scale. "It's gone from the RPF against the Rwandan army, to multi-faction chaos between tribes and clans with a history of hate and violence against each other."

"Africa in a bloody nutshell," Stewart mused.

King checked his watch. "We've got four and a half hours to do this, and get back to the taxi," he said, realising how crazy it sounded to be taxied to and from a raid. "David is going to take off after that, and we'll be stuck in the middle of nowhere and out of options."

"We have a secondary helicopter exfil," said Stewart, checking his watch. "Which means we still have a lift out of here in three hours, but it's five miles southwest of the plantation, and that is going to be a push in this terrain, and we still haven't even got Bentuwi out yet. The problem is that the chopper is part of our deal with a new Ugandan government. Someone with some clout will make it disappear with air traffic control. No Bentuwi, then no ride out of here. If the pilot sees us without him, then he'll take off without us."

King stood up. "Well, we're not going to get out of this fucking place if we're just chin-wagging here, so we'd better get moving..."

"That means crossing back over the river." Stewart paused. "I've only just crossed. That's twice, I will have used all my luck up..."

King shrugged. "Well, you've already done it twice before and you've still got both your legs..." King studied the water, taking in the opposite bank. "Oh, fuck it..." he said and leapt into the water. He surfaced, cradling the rifle and sculled on his back until he reached the shallows.

"Goddamm it..." Stewart said, muttering a string of expletives under his breath and he followed. When he looked up at King he was aiming his rifle at the water. Stewart kicked for grim death, struggling up the bank and falling onto his belly. Aware that he was in no way clear of danger, he ran, zig-zagging until he reached King, who lowered the rifle. "How close was it to me?"

"What?"

"The crocodile..." he said, turning and looking at the water. "How close was it?"

King grinned. "I was just fucking with you, boss."

Stewart stared at him as he shook his head. "Aye, you really are a bastard's bastard, King..."

# Chapter Thirty
## DAILY MAIL By Mark Larcombe, foreign affairs correspondent

Communities across Rwanda are facing escalating violence that regional observers warn could spiral into mass atrocities if urgent international action is not taken. The clashes—rooted in long-standing ethnic, political, and territorial tensions—have driven thousands of families from their homes in recent days, raising fears of a looming humanitarian emergency.

Villages caught in the crossfire between the Rwandan military forces and Rwandan rebels have emptied almost overnight, with survivors fleeing towards neighbouring countries in search of safety. Aid workers say the scale and speed of displacement are already stretching regional resources to the limit. Several border authorities are reporting that makeshift camps are appearing faster than they can be supported, prompting calls for coordinated relief efforts.

Officials on the ground emphasise that the movement of people is not a "crisis of migration," but a crisis of survival. Families are travelling with little more than what they can carry, often separated from loved ones and without access to food, water, or medical care. International agencies warn that without immediate intervention—including protection for civilians and support for overburdened host communities—the situation could deteriorate further.

Governments across the region and in Europe are watching developments closely as fears for mass migration following the wars in Iraq and Afghanistan and the rising of the Arab Spring have put a strain on borders and aid. Diplomatic pressure is mounting for a ceasefire and renewed peace talks, while humanitarian organisations urge donor nations to prepare for increased support needs in the coming weeks.

For the millions living in the affected areas, however, the priority is stark and immediate: safety, stability, and the hope that the world will not look away.

# Chapter Thirty-One
## Dakar, Senegal

The ocean shimmied in the African sun, casting reflections across the coastline of Dakar. Overhead, rolling clouds tinged orange by Saharan dust drifted lazily, remnants of the earlier rainfall evident in the red residue now drying on whitewashed walls and the cars parked in the street below. In the faded glow of afternoon, the city moved with a languid energy, as if the heat and dust weighed on every step. Children played football in alleyways, their laughter echoing against the backdrop of distant traffic and the rhythmic call of street vendors. The air, thick and warm, carried the scent of salt and spices, mingling with the earthy aroma of wet dust that clung to every surface.

From a shaded balcony of the hotel bar, the city's contradictions became clear. Gleaming new buildings stood beside colonial relics, and the hustle of daily life continued even as news of chaos to the east filtered through radio static. Life in Dakar, for now, unfolded in a fragile peace, the city both a sanctuary and a reminder of the storm gathering beyond its borders.

**Crossfire**

Richard Collins watched the surfers vying for waves. Slick black bodies paddling colourful boards through the water, chasing the swells before they broke lazily and washed onto the sand. These were locals surfing what little they had; not travelling surfers in search of the perfect wave. He had not surfed in years, not since his days spent living in Durban, and he yearned to experience the juxtaposed calm and thrill once more. Another time, perhaps. Right now, he had more to deal with than simple pleasures. The vibrating phone broke his thoughts, and he checked the caller ID before answering, even though it could only have been from one person. Typical of Preet Du Plessis, he had waited for Collins to ring off before returning the man's call.

*"Result, my friend!"* Preet Du Plessis greeted him.

Collins smiled to himself. He had not given a single thought to the three hundred and thirty souls killed along with his target, and nor had he lost any sleep over the million and counting Rwandans slaughtered in the uprising. "It went like clockwork..." he replied proudly.

*"Where are you now?"*

"Ghana," he lied. Collins trusted Du Plessis, but only up to a point. However, he did not trust mobile phones at all and would ditch this one as soon as he had finished this conversation. For this reason, he had not made the call from his own hotel where his phone could be potentially located, instead choosing one on the seafront with a busy coffee bar.

*"My advice would be to get out of Africa for a while. Your old employers will want to even the score, so distance will be your friend until it dies down."*

Collins laughed. "Civil wars don't tend to die down too quickly, bru..."

*"I'll wire you some money when you find somewhere to hole up. I suggest we give it six months for the dust to settle*

*and for the British intelligence services to trip over their own feet looking for you, and then I will have some very interesting contracts for you to fulfil."* Preet Du Plessis chuckled. *"I guarantee it, my friend. Where will you go?"*

"Italy," he lied. He had no intention of going there, but until he got a new phone and secured his base, then he would keep the man in the dark until he wired him his money.

*"Then until we meet again, arrivederci!"*

Collins ended the call, took off the back of the phone and removed both the SIM card and the battery. He snapped the SIM and dropped one half over the balcony and the other into the planter beside him. He would ditch the phone and battery into the sea as he returned to his hotel along the seafront. It was belt and braces, but he preferred to be thorough. He gazed out over the ocean, watching as the foaming whitewater broke along the shore. The idea of living somewhere he could see the sea every day appealed to him. Europe presented itself as a tempting prospect—a straightforward journey up the coast by bus and train, passing through Morocco, before catching a ferry across to Cádiz in Spain. The continent's efficient rail and bus networks, coupled with the myriad of ferries criss-crossing the Mediterranean, would make travel easy and discreet. The Greek islands held a particular allure. Their rich history, luminous skies, and brilliant azure waters had always captured his imagination. There, nestled among ancient ruins and sunlit villages, he could disappear. MI6 would not find him if he kept off the grid and embraced a simple, unremarkable existence for the next six months. The prospect sent a thrill through him, a mixture of anticipation and relief. With these thoughts swirling in his mind,

**Crossfire**

he finished his coffee, left a modest tip for the waitress, and made his way back towards his hotel, determined to put his plan into motion.

# Chapter Thirty-Two
## THE TIMES By our Foreign Correspondent, Jon Trainor.

In the heart of Central Africa, the spectre of civil war has once again descended upon Rwanda already scarred by decades of unrest. Towns and villages, once vibrant with the hum of daily life, now echo with the sharp retort of gunfire and the mournful wails of those displaced. The rapid, violent advance of armed factions through the dense forests and across the savannah has left thousands fleeing their homes, seeking refuge wherever it may be found. The confirmed death toll stands at around 329,000 deaths in the first two days but estimates that have been made at more than a million have yet to be independently verified.

The latest outbreak of violence erupted after a fragile peace accord collapsed under the weight of political infighting and deep-seated ethnic divisions, was thrown into disarray after the assassination of Rwanda President, Kwizari Habimana along with twenty-seven members of the Rwandan trade delegation en route to Mali for the Food and Agriculture Organisation (FAO) which holds a conference every two years for member countries in Africa to

## Crossfire

discuss the region's food and agricultural challenges and priorities. Rwanda Airline's Flight WB-701 was destroyed by a surface to air missile seven miles from Bamako International Airport, killing three hundred and thirty-two souls onboard. Exiled political activist Motu Manasi, a council member of the Rwandan Patriotic Front claimed responsibility with several news outlets, including the *BBC World Service* in the minutes before the tragedy. Motu Manasi and other RPF followers are believed to have been hiding out in Uganda before crossing into Rwanda to lead rebel forces.

Reports from the ground suggest that government forces and rebel militias have both been implicated in atrocities, with civilians bearing the brunt of the conflict caught between government forces and warring factions with long-standing disputes.

In the capital, smoke rises from the embattled districts, and humanitarian agencies warn of a looming humanitarian crisis as food supplies dwindle and medical services are stretched beyond breaking point. International observers have called for calm and renewed dialogue, but with trust in short supply and old grievances festering, hopes for an immediate resolution appear remote. The United Nations has appealed for greater international assistance, while neighbouring states brace for a potential spill-over of violence. Meanwhile, the people of Central Africa endure another chapter of fear and uncertainty, their lives once more dictated by the caprices of war.

As the world watches, *The Times* remains committed to bringing the stories of those caught in the crossfire to the fore. In the words of one exhausted refugee, "We have lost so much, but we cannot afford to lose hope." It is a hope that, for now, flickers faintly amid the chaos.

## Chapter Thirty-Three
### Uganda

They found the bodies of two Ugandan soldiers peppered with bullet holes as they drew near to the summit of the hill. To avoid detection, King and Stewart had strayed further into the jungle away from the previously cultivated land between the jungle and the plantation. King relieved one of the bodies of a bandolier and filled it with magazines from both dead soldiers. He handed two magazines to Stewart, who was staring intently into the brush.

"What's up?" he asked.

"I've found Chris," Stewart said heavily.

King followed the man's stare, then trudged further up the slope to where Chris was leaning, as if resting peacefully, against the thick trunk of a tree. He was sitting down, legs outstretched, his head bowed. There was blood soaked down his shirt, a bullet hole to his right side, close to his liver. King noticed the bullet wounds to the man's legs. His rifle rested beside him, and it was clear that he had made it this far, unable to go any further. His last act had been to take down both soldiers as they drew near, then most likely ebbed into unconsciousness from blood loss. King bent down and removed the man's 9mm Browning and two grenades from his webbing. His last act, before returning to Stewart, was to close the man's eyes.

"If we don't break Moffusa Bentuwi out, then I want to kill as many of these fuckers as we can," Stewart said coldly. "No mercy, no fucking surrender…"

"No. Fuck that, boss. I don't know these guys, so I'm not on a bloody vendetta. We either get Bentuwi out and get the hell out of here, or if we can't get the man out, then we melt away into the landscape…" He paused. "Just like you taught me…"

"I fucking hate it when you're right…"

King grinned at the compliment, his eyes alert as he scanned the terrain ahead. Pausing for a moment, he assessed the ground, ensuring there were no hidden dangers or signs of enemy movement. Once satisfied, he motioned for Stewart to follow and took the lead, moving cautiously towards the edge of the jungle. The dense foliage gave way to open ground marked by terraced slopes, exposing them to potential threats from above and below.

As soon as King reached the fringe of the jungle and the open expanse of the terraces, he dropped flat onto his stomach. With deliberate care, he pressed himself into the mud, moving forward inch by inch. Using just his elbows, knees, and toes, he inched his way across the exposed ground, every muscle tensed and ready. His rifle, held securely in the crook of his elbows, never wavered from its position, ready at a moment's notice. Behind him, Stewart mirrored his actions, both men acutely aware that the slightest mistake could reveal their position and mean certain death.

As King and Stewart watched from their concealed position, their worst fears materialised before them.

Soldiers, moving in coordinated groups of four or six, were being meticulously briefed before fanning out into the jungle. The officer in charge was a striking figure—overweight, draped in sashes, and wielding a baton with an air of authority reminiscent of a British officer from the era spanning the Victorian Empire to the Second World War. His presence, coupled with the disciplined organisation of the troops, underscored the gravity of the situation: the enemy was not only well-armed but also well-led and alert to the possibility of intruders in their midst. There was a good possibility that the officer had been trained at Sandhurst, the idea being that Britain's allies had officers with a good standard of training, and that would cascade down the ranks. Of course, this often did not happen, or got lost in translation, and the average soldier throughout the African continent joined up merely for three meals a day, a bed at night and some pay at the end of the month. He wasn't renowned for his professionalism, although so far, two highly trained ex-special forces soldiers had fallen, and a third had been captured, so as far as King was concerned, all bets were off.

"The more men he sends into the jungle, then the less there will be to fight when we get down there," Stewart said decisively.

"*If* we get down there," King commented sardonically. He pointed half-way down the terraces, a lot further out from cover. "We can lay up there and see what's what." He paused. "From there, we can sprint if we have to, get into the plantation house and if we can get hold of Bentuwi, then it's a straight sprint down the sago slopes to the river."

"And the crocs..." Stewart said quietly.

"Fourth time lucky, eh?"

King took the lead, moving with deliberate caution

through the exposed terrain. He understood that Stewart would keep a safe distance behind, ready to react if they came under sudden attack. If anyone were to open fire on them, Stewart would have the space and time to return fire or seek cover, rather than being caught in the same line of fire as King. Every step King took was measured and controlled; he avoided any rapid or abrupt movements, knowing that such actions could easily catch the eye of a watchful enemy. Stewart, who had always referred to this approach as 'brazening it out', understood the necessity of King's steady, composed advance. Together, their movements demonstrated a disciplined approach to remaining undetected in hostile territory.

King got down behind some thick bushes that he thought was camomile. They provided good cover, but only from view. He would have preferred something that stopped bullets, merely than just prying eyes. King shouldered the rifle, estimating the distance to be two hundred and fifty metres. The weapon was only furnished with iron sights – a post on the fore end and a ghost ring, or peep-sight on the rear – but he could see the overweight officer in them quite clearly. Surrounding the officer were the last six soldiers, all that remained from the original force of more than thirty men. This number was excessive for the purposes of guarding a secret prison and considerably larger than the enemy presence King had noted during his initial reconnaissance. The dwindling numbers made it clear that the jungle and fields were now full of soldiers hunting for them, and they could only have reacted to a tip-off, and King could not get it out of his head that the tip-off could only have come from Collins.

"What are you doing?" Steward whispered as he crouched down beside him.

"Seeing if the shot is makeable."

"Are you mad?"

"It's makeable."

"I fucking trained you, lad. I know it's makeable." Stewart paused. "But there's two NCOs and six men down there as well as that fat colonel, and you won't make all those shots with iron sights."

"What's *your* plan, then?"

# Chapter Thirty-Four
## Rwanda

Smoke filled the streets, and with it, the sickly-sweet stench of roasted meats. The tyres still burned fiercely, and the corpses of the poor souls who had been secured by the tyres with their arms pinned to their waists before being doused in petrol and set ablaze still smouldered on the ground. The aftermath of a crowd incited and a culture under perceived threat had laid an indelible image on the soul of the journalist as she scoured the streets for a story. The *Who? What?* and *Why?* That was crucial to every story. That would be woven into the obvious scene of death and destruction. That was what made her great, when others simply recorded and reported sensationalism peppered with fact. Lucinda Davenport knew all about what made a good story, and what made a great one, and once she had discovered the formula, she sought only to report the facts in a way that hit her viewers between the eyes and jarred their insides. It did not make her reports breaking news, but it *did* make her reports both memorable and sparked the consciousness of her audience.

By now, the world knew that the Rwandan president had been killed, and that more than three hundred and thirty people had lost their lives as collateral damage in the crash. News agencies had flooded the screens and papers with images of death and destruction, and experts had given their take on what the rebels wished to achieve, and what the leaderless government would do next, and whether the military would assume rule until the rebels were beaten and a new leader could be appointed. Rwanda was undergoing a sea change, and the future of the region was uncertain. Close to a million people were now thought to have perished in ethnic cleansing and tribal and cultural feuds on both sides, most of the people slain with agricultural tools and machetes as old scores were settled. Within two days the rivers were filled with bodies, the waters running red as crocodiles fed on the dead, hyenas and wild dogs scavenged on the riverbanks, and entire ethnicities were washed away, or their remains scattered across the land.

The majority Hutu tribes had battled ferociously with the Rwandan government forces, with the Tutsi joining forces with the Hutu and the Twa attacked and killed by all. The status quo was changing far too quickly for any chance of peace to be established, and in the highlands the Tutsi and Hutu were still intent on killing each other rather than strike an accord. The government forces simply killed anybody carrying a weapon or standing in their way, and that extended to women and children, with many people on all sides having limbs cut off to serve as a reminder of the side they should have chosen. Only yesterday morning, Lucinda and her team had come across the aftermath of the Rwandan national soccer team whose coach had been forced off the road and every man's right leg hacked off above the knee, the manager and coach having both forearms amputated by machetes. It was, as tended to be the case in Africa, brutality in the extreme and she was sure that she would be haunted by the sight for evermore.

Lucinda looked down at the child in her arms. She did not know whether the child was a boy or a girl, and there did not seem reason to look, but the child was wrapped in what she could only describe as swaddling clothes, because the wraps of cloth covering the child from head to toe secured them so tightly, so comfortingly, that they had not been hurt by the fall to the ground as their mother had been felled with a rifle butt, raped by multiple men, and slaughtered afterwards with machetes. It was obvious to Lucinda what had happened, and she struggled to understand just how neighbour could abuse neighbour to such a horrifying degree. Civil war was unfathomable. How genocide could spark from the tiniest ember, spreading like wildfire through a sun-baked pine forest.

Lucinda's experience as a journalist extended far beyond the current horrors she now witnessed in Rwanda. Her career had previously taken her to the heart of the Balkan wars, although her role then was one step removed from the immediate dangers of conflict. From the relative safety of her townhouse in Kensington or the bustling offices on Fleet Street, she had focused on the meticulous work of fact-checking and editing reports sent in by correspondents embedded in Croatia, Kosovo, or Bosnia. Despite the physical distance from the violence, the stories of brutality that crossed her desk left a profound impact, haunting her during restless, sleepless nights. The atrocities committed during those wars remained vivid in her memory, a constant reminder of the cost of conflict even for those who only observed it at a distance.

"What are we going to do with her?" Lucinda asked,

looking at the body of the child's mother lying lifeless and degraded on the ground.

"They'll blur out her bits in the edit," Ian Gallagher said, checking his camera.

"Ian!" Malcolm Selby exclaimed. "I'm sure Lucinda meant the woman's body..."

"I did, thank you Malcolm."

Gallagher shrugged. "A million people have been slaughtered, Lucinda. There's nobody to call, and even if we did, they may well be the same people who did this." He paused. "There's a sheet of plastic over there by the car..." He pointed to an old Peugeot that was jacked up on bricks with the wheels removed. "We can cover her up with that, but we really need to address the big fucking question, and that's what to do with the kid..."

"There's the orphanage in Tanzania..." Lucinda said. "And it would make an incredible story. An orphaned war child taken to safety."

"You're kidding..." Malcolm Selby stared at her, then at the swaddled child in her arms.

"Do I look like I'm kidding?" she replied indignantly.

"Lucinda, who are we to assume that the child is orphaned? Yes, his mother is tragically dead, but he or she may have a father, siblings, grandparents or aunts or uncles," Selby protested. "We need to take the child to the authorities..."

"Who could very well have done this themselves! These bastards could have been Rwandan military for all we know!" Lucinda shook her head dejectedly.

Selby shrugged. "I know... I guess there's nothing between these people. They're *all* bloody animals..."

"Your *Guardian* reading, Notting Hill chums wouldn't like you saying that, Malcolm," Gallagher chided.

## Crossfire

"Oh, fuck off, Ian," Selby replied tiresomely.

Ian Gallagher laughed. "Oh, come on, Malcolm! Look around you. Do you see any signs of humanity? Other than what Lucinda is suggesting, that is..."

Lucinda rocked the child as they started to protest, already missing its mother and the thought that they never would remember her tore through her insides. The world could be such a cruel place, and as a journalist she only ever seemed to see the worst of it. She shushed the child comfortingly, already thinking of them as a girl because of the delicate features. The child would need to eat soon. Or would *she* need milk? Lucinda could only guess at her age, and there were any number of factors that contribute to the child appearing smaller and younger than they really were. She figured that the mother had swaddled the child for ease, and the loose lengths of fabric would likely have wrapped and tied around her mother to make a papoose, leaving her hands free to carry water. An upturned bucket and a patch of damp earth around it pointed to that being the case.

"Shit, Lucinda... there's a truckful of soldiers coming..." Malcolm Selby said, looking over her shoulder.

The three of them wore blue flak jackets over their shirts with 'PRESS' printed in bold, white lettering front and back. Lucinda glanced over her shoulder, her heart missing a beat when she saw the green pickup truck laden with men, with a heavy machine gun mounted in the bed of the truck and bullet holes and pock marks in the bodywork.

"Government forces," said Gallagher, almost hopefully but not sure why. In their short time in the country, they had seen atrocities from all four sides. "Just remain calm, guys," he added, but his tone would suggest that it was for his own benefit as much as his colleagues.

The truck drew to a halt and three men leapt out of the

rear, with one man remaining being the belt-fed machine gun. The driver got out and lit an own-rolled cigarette and a large man stepped out from the passenger side smoking a fat cigar. The large man wore a thick belt over an ample gut, and his chest bore insignia and medals that indicated that he was in charge. As he walked towards them, he pulled on a pair of mirrored aviators and made a big show of smoking the cigar as if he were a boardroom plutocrat. In a final act of absurd signalling, he rubbed his stomach in a manner that made Lucinda think that he wore his obesity as a badge of both pride and privilege in a country where many people struggled to feed their families.

"Who are you people?" he barked in the tone of someone who was used to getting what he wanted through rank and intimidation alone. "Why are you in my country?"

"I am Lucinda Davenport, news correspondent for..."

"Be quiet, whore!" the man snapped, turning to both men. "Who are you?"

Lucinda looked stunned at such blatant misogyny and sexism, but before she could protest Malcolm Selby placed a hand on her arm and said, "This is Lucinda Davenport, my name is Malcolm Selby, and this is Ian Gallagher. We are news journalist, producer and editor, and cameraman, respectively." He paused. "We have visas and media passes, and you are required to allow us the freedom to report these terrible events without prejudice or obstruction." He smiled warmly and added, "And who are you, if I may ask?"

"Colonel Jones..." the man smirked.

"Colonel Jones?" Selby frowned. He was used to the contrast of names and languages throughout the African continent, but Jones seemed unlikely at best.

"There has been many terrible atrocities in the war so

far..." Lucinda said calmly. "If the rest of the world knows the truth, becomes emotionally and ethically involved in this conflict, then pressure will mount for a peaceful resolution. Our report, and reports from other media teams like us, could end the war and stop the slaughter of innocent people..."

"You know these people?" Colonel Jones presented a hand towards the bodies in the background, the body of the child's mother on the ground beside Lucinda. "Scum," he said. "Tutsi scum. They contribute nothing, are worth nothing..."

Lucinda tensed, and without glancing at her two colleagues, she sensed their reaction, too. These men were not fighting to help these people – they were mopping up.

"Give me the child," the man said.

"No." She thought her voice belonged to a third party, because she wasn't thinking, wasn't in control anymore.

The man stepped forwards and snatched the child from her, gripping the swaddling clothes as if the child were a bag of grain or potatoes. He cradled the child in his arms and looked into their eyes. For a moment, there seemed to be a connection and Lucinda wondered whether her heartbeat would indeed subside and everything was going to be alright. She glanced at Selby, who gave a brief nod mirroring her thoughts, and then almost at once, her producer's expression seemed otherworldly. His eyes went wide, his colour drained and if Lucinda could ever have imagined a man's soul ripped from him by demons, the life drained from him in an instant, then Malcolm Selby's face was all of those things and more. Time seemed to stand still, and as she forced herself to look back towards the big Rwandan and the helpless child, she felt all the things she had witnessed in Selby's face tear through her soul. The gunshot echoed around her, rather than penetrating her ears at such close range, and the blood and brain and bone splattered in her face as she watched the soldier drop the bundle onto the ground. When she finally tore her eyes away from the horror, she looked up into the man's face, and his beaming, wicked grin.

Everything else became a blur. Rough hands upon her, the shouts of protest from Selby and Gallagher, the screams from both of them – fearful and agonising all at once – the way the colonel dragged her over the rubble and into the hut then threw her to the ground. He clothes were torn from her, and she felt ashamed that she did not fight back, was too frightened to flee, and that somehow felt worse than the pain and indignity of what the big man did next. When it was over – time seemed to stand still and rush by all at once, and she could not tell if it had been mere seconds or agonisingly slow minutes – she lay on her back and watched as he buttoned his clothes, all the while grinning at her. Again, the man's smile seemed worse than what he had done to her, indescribable humiliation.

Lucinda lay there as she heard voices and vehicle doors and eventually, the pickup truck drive away. As she dressed, it felt as if she were having an out-of-body-experience, a nightmare that she could not rouse herself from. It wasn't happening, hadn't happened to her. And yet, as she wiped herself with her torn underwear and pulled on her jeans and shirt, buttoning what few buttons remained, there was no escape from the fact that it *was* her, and it *had* happened, and if she lived long enough to make it home, then her life would never be the same again.

When she finally pulled on enough strength to get to her feet, she staggered out of the hut and squinted through the glaring sunlight and limped out into the open. It was not just the obvious discomfort, but her back and neck and legs stabbed with pain, her body beaten and forced to comply with her attacker's wants and needs. She had once taken a nasty fall on ice while skiing in St. Moritz and her body had hurt everywhere at once, but that memory paled into insignificance with what she had just endured. Lucinda steadied herself on the vehicle jacked up on bricks and waited for her eyes to adjust to the light. Her equilibrium was off kilter, but as she looked towards their vehicle, the bundle of blood-soaked swaddling clothes sobered her at once. Only the muffled cries coming from behind the vehicle made her look away from the horror, and she limped towards the sound, already fearful at what she might find.

Malcolm was leaning against the large off-road tyre of the vehicle, cradling his right arm which he had wrapped in his jacket. His breathing was ragged, and when he looked up at her he sobbed, "They cut off my hand..."

The words stabbed through her like a shard of ice. She went to him and tried to help, but he would not release his grip on the wrapped stump, blood soaked into the material and dripping onto the ground. Ian's wails made her look thankfully away, and she saw her cameraman limping towards her, cradling his right arm, the end of the bleeding stump wrapped in his own blood-soaked shirt.

Lucinda ran to him, wrapped an arm around his shoulder and helped him back to the vehicle. The man's anguished sobs and cries filled the air, and though she was still reeling from her own ordeal, she found that focusing on the immediate task of helping her injured companions was the only thing keeping her from breaking down completely. In a way, tending to their wounds—however selfish it might have seemed—gave her mind something else to hold onto, a distraction from the horror she had just endured. With every step, she concentrated on supporting Ian's weight and guiding him towards the vehicle, determined to get both him and Malcolm the medical attention they so desperately needed.

## Chapter Thirty-Five

They could hear the screams from outside the building, and the sound was enough to chill them to the bone. Stewart stepped past King, but he gripped the tough Scotsman tightly by his arm and pulled him back.

"Fools rush in, remember?" King hissed at him.

Stewart scowled. It had been one of his mantras, and at the sound of his old friend's agony, he had been about to forget the training that he had instilled in so many soldiers and MI6 recruits over the years. "Cheeky bastard..." he growled.

King slung the rifle over his shoulder, the weight of it a familiar burden, yet in the cramped confines of the corridor it was more hindrance than help. With his left hand, he drew his knife, the blade glinting in the muted light, ready for close combat should it come to that. In his right hand, he gripped the 9mm pistol, its compact frame far more suited to the narrow passageway than the cumbersome FN FAL rifle. He was acutely aware of the limitations of his weaponry in such tight quarters; the long rifle, once a staple of Western armies, had since been abandoned for lighter, shorter, and less powerful systems that offered greater manoeuvrability. Now, with the odds stacked against him and every decision a matter of survival, King relied on the tools best suited to the immediate threat, moving forward with calculated resolve.

"Watch the door," King told him. "I'll go on ahead..."

Stewart would have preferred to go forward, but his protégé was right. The last thing they needed was to be boxed in front and back, and half the damn army could return while they were moving through the corridor and then there would be no escape. Stewart stepped inside the corridor a couple of paces, then turned and crouched down, his weapon shouldered and the muzzle resting near the ground ready to bring to aim if necessary.

King moved cautiously through the corridor, following the direction of the harrowing screams. His palms were slick with nervous sweat, and his mouth had gone completely dry—a familiar response that always seemed to grip him in moments like this. The sensations were as much a part of him as his training; the physical tells of the adrenaline surging through his system. He noted the contrast; in quieter, safer times, his body would have been relaxed and at ease, but now every sense was heightened, every muscle tense, as he prepared himself for whatever might be waiting around the next corner. The two guards stood lazily chatting, quite unfazed by the noises of a man being tortured for information. King surged forwards, slicing one of the guards across the throat with the blade and driving the butt of the pistol into the other man's temple. The man wasn't out cold, and would soon regain his senses, but not after King drove his boot with fourteen stone behind it, down onto the man's face. The other guard was close to bleeding out, and King

## Crossfire

removed the man's Uzi sub-machinegun and tucked his own pistol away before checking the open breech and flicking off the safety. He retrieved a bunch of keys from the man's belt and slipped them into his pocket. When he looked back down at the man, his eyes were glazed and staring blankly back at him in the way that only death could.

King checked the open hatch in the metal door. Despite its outward appearance as a plantation house, the building's interior was unmistakably that of a prison. The door to the cell, heavy and reinforced, resembled those found in police stations and prisons across the world. Yet, the chilling screams emanating from within belonged not to a typical holding cell, but to a clandestine prison reserved for Uganda's political detainees. The unsettling contrast between the genteel façade and the brutal reality behind the door was stark. Here, the architecture served as a cruel disguise, masking the horrors endured by those trapped inside. King could see Paddy strapped to a chair, the electrodes clipped to his nipples and genitals, blood smeared on his face and chest, and a pool of water at his feet. There were three men inside. One doing the asking, and two doing the hurting. One of the men doused the former SAS soldier with water, while the other twisted the dial that controlled the current coming off the car battery. It was a harrowing sight, but King bypassed the door and concentrated on the objective. Paddy was a big boy, and he had known the score going into this. King would free him if he could, but right now, the man's screams were a welcome diversion that would provide him with the cover he would need.

The next two cells yielded nothing more than four broken men who paid King little attention through the hatch. Their eyes were glazed and yellowed from malaria, and their sagging skin and loose, tattered clothing showed they had lost weight. King continued down the corridor and checked two locked doors that did not have observation hatches. The first of the two locked doors opened into a cluttered storeroom; its shelves lined with miscellaneous supplies and items of little immediate use. The second door presented more of a challenge, secured by two separate locks—one mounted high, the other set low. King paused momentarily, weighing up his options before using the retrieved keys to unlock the door. Inside, he discovered a cache of arms and ammunition. King surveyed the available weaponry, his eyes immediately drawn to a box of fragmentation grenades and metal boxes containing cardboard cartons of various calibres of ammunition. He quickly pocketed two grenades and two cartons 7.62x51mm ammunition, which he slipped into the pouches on the bandolier hanging across his chest.

There was a bored looking guard outside a cell up ahead, and King ducked back around the corner as he decided the best course of action. His skin colour would make him stick out like a sore thumb and he couldn't hope to approach on any kind of pretence. However, opening fire with an Uzi in the confines of the corridor would bring anybody within a hundred metres running. King drew the knife and checked the weight and balance, deciding to hold it by the handle. That would mean that he would have to take at least six paces before throwing it. As a loose rule – and King had found many knives to not listen to the rule – a throw from three, nine and twelve paces required him to hold the tip of the blade. From four and eight paces, holding the handle worked well. Beyond twelve paces, King had always found the arc too great. With a Fairburn & Sykes commando dagger, he had perfected the 'dart throw', using his index finger against the guard to spin the knife clockwise like a bullet as it left his grip in a straight, arrow-like throw, sending it to the target up to fifteen metres away. He already knew that the sheath knife in his hand would need a rotating throw, but he included a fail-safe in that he would throw hard enough that if the handle should impact first, then it would do so with significant force enough to stun his enemy.

King eased out from around the corner and walked steadily towards the guard. As the man turned, King quickened his pace and lengthened his stride, then drew back the knife towards his shoulder and hurled it with all his might. The knife spun three complete rotations and struck the guard in his chest as he turned to face the threat. The blade buried itself halfway through the breastbone, and King charged forwards and struck the pommel with the palm of his hand, driving the blade a full seven inches deep, up to the hilt. King caught hold of the guard's neck and tripped his feet, dropping him to the floor, then pulled the blade clear and watched as the blood gushed from the man's aorta. The guard's eyes glazed, and his ragged breathing went still as he exhaled. King wiped both sides of the blade on the man's sleeve and sheathed the knife before peering through the hatch.

Moffusa Bentuwi sat on a single bunk in the bare concrete cell, his only company a toilet and a sink. The harshness of the environment was unmistakable; King had endured far worse conditions himself and knew what it meant to be confined in such a place. For Bentuwi, held without trial and denied any prospect of release, the confinement would have been a relentless torment, a living hell. Yet, Bentuwi remained unbroken. His demeanour revealed a blend of acceptance and quiet confidence, a stark contrast to the despair and defeat that marked so many others in the prison. King had taken note of this during his earlier reconnaissance, observing that Bentuwi's spirit had not been crushed by his ordeal. Unlike the other prisoners, who bore visible signs of suffering and hopelessness, Bentuwi appeared resilient and composed, his resolve undiminished by his captivity. King knew that this was testament to the man, Uganda's true leader, but for the de facto president who had the support from military leaders because of General Mantutsi's power and reach. King had ended that, and now it would be down to Moffusa Bentuwi to garner support from the citizens of Uganda and get the military onside.

King tried a couple of keys before the lock yielded. The Ugandan regarded him curiously, not moving from the bed. "Please stand, Mr Bentuwi..."

"Who are you?"

"I'm getting you out."

"On whose payroll?"

King frowned. "Does it matter?"

"It matters very much."

King grabbed hold of the man by the scruff of his neck, his shirt tearing as he pulled him easily to his feet. "Men have died for me to get this far," King growled.

"I won't be a puppet for a country hanging on to the notion of a colonial empire," Bentuwi said quietly. "I have my beliefs, and I have a dream of what is possible for the people of this nation, and what this nation can achieve." The man paused. "The British Empire is no more. If I were to be president, I would seek to leave the British Commonwealth." He shrugged. "You had just as well know my intentions *before* you risk your life any further to free me."

"Thankfully, that's all above my pay scale," King

replied, pulling the man with him to the door. "Fucking hell, I thought you'd *want* to be free..."

"I am free. Free in mind, if not in body," he replied pointedly. "They can lock me away, they can hold me in chains, but they will never take my freedom..."

"Jesus wept, I bet you've been annoying as fuck..." King quipped. "We may just walk out of here without a fight if the guards think they're getting rid of you..." He pulled Bentuwi with him, his right hand gripping the Uzi firmly, the muzzle trained in front of him at waist level. King favoured the Uzi sub-machinegun in close quarters. It needed all the skill to operate at close range as a child spraying a water pistol.

Several gunshots echoed down the corridor, and King knew that the chances of walking out of here without a fight was no longer a reality. As he rounded the corner, the two men who had been torturing Paddy were stepping out of the cell. Both men were unarmed, as was interrogation protocol, and stepped into a hail of 9mm bullets from two short bursts of fire from the Uzi.

"You murdered them! They were unarmed!" Bentuwi protested, his words echoing down the corridor.

King pushed the man to the ground and kicked open the door. King shot the interrogator in his face, then dropped the empty weapon on the ground before drawing the pistol. He ripped off the crocodile clips off Paddy's nipples and used his knife to slice through the rope securing the man's wrists.

"Can you walk?" he asked, looking at the blood-soaked bandage on wrapping the man's thigh.

"I'll fucking well crawl if I have to..." the Irishman replied.

King handed him his pistol and unslung his rifle. "On

me, then..." He pulled Bentuwi to his feet and dragged him with him. It was a struggle to wield the heavy rifle with just one hand, but he wasn't about to trade a rifle for a pistol now that they had been compromised. There were more gunshots, and King saw Stewart crouching low and firing his weapon from the doorway.

"Eight men, two down!" the Scotsman shouted as he reached him. "Lay down some more fire and I think they'll run..."

King pushed Bentuwi to the ground and risked a peek. He could see men moving sixty metres away beside a low wall and he emptied the magazine of twenty rounds at them before hastily reloading. He kept the empty magazine, remembering the two cartons of ammunition that he had taken. Stewart set about firing off his twenty rounds in double and triple taps, and as soon as he ducked back inside to reload, King tossed a fragmentation grenade their way, then followed up with a smoke grenade to cover their dash for escape.

"On me! On me!" he shouted and ran outside, ducking to his left and leaving it up to Stewart to handle Bentuwi. Paddy was a big boy and could handle himself, but right now, King did not want to risk becoming bogged down in a building that the enemy forces would eventually surround and control. Once that happened then they could be flushed out with fire, pummelled with gunfire and ordinance – or even starved out.

King hit the ground beside a low wall and rolled over to see Stewart running with Bentuwi in his grip, and Paddy limping behind firing single shots through the smoke at an unseen enemy. A waste of precious ammunition, but a tactic that could buy them some time as the enemy ducked the sound of gunshots. King aimed his rifle a few feet past

## Crossfire

Paddy and fired half a dozen rounds into the smoke, before rolling back onto his front and resting in a crouch. "Left is east, and east is our exfil..." he said loudly enough for the two men to hear above the gunfire. He tossed his last magazine for the pistol to Paddy and changed to a new magazine himself, pocketing the partially used one. He now had twenty-one rounds left in his rifle. It was moments like these that made it clear to him why the British military had chosen to move on from the old cumbersome rifles, opting instead for lighter weapons equipped with standard thirty-round magazines. Even so, as someone who'd experienced his fair share of close quarter battles, King knew all too well that in the heat of battle it never truly felt like enough ammunition, no matter what sort of firepower you carried.

King led the way again. It wasn't bravery. In his experience it was more likely that the second or third person to move got the bullet. The first in line merely alerted the enemy. When he reached a stone outbuilding and turned to give covering fire for Stewart, his theory was proved correct as he watched Paddy go down. He had seen enough death to know that there was no saving him, and he fired a few rounds to give Stewart and Bentuwi the cover they needed.

They had reached the edge of the plantation's grounds. From here, it was slopes and terraces of sago, tea, coffee and maize. The crops would not provide much in the way of suitable cover, but the jungle was not far away, and once they were out of sight, then the scales would balance once more. King started running but almost ran into three soldiers who stepped out from the lee of the building, and unwittingly into his path. He fired the rifle from waist level, taking two of them to the ground, and shoulder barged the third, who fought back wildly, dropping his own weapon in the fall and flailing his arms and legs, hammering blows into

King's face. King landed heavily on his back, but he caught hold of the man's lapels and bench pressed him into the air, his head exploding into a crimson mist as Stewart fired a single shot from his rifle.

As King scrambled to his feet, two more gunshots rang out as Stewart finished off the other two soldiers on the ground, much to the disgust of Bentuwi, who protested loudly.

"Oh, we've got a right one here, boss," said King. "Doesn't want an alliance with Britain, wants to withdraw from the Commonwealth, doesn't want his captors killed…" he said, taking a CZ75 9mm pistol from one of the bodies, then tucking it into his waistband. "Doesn't seem to give a shit that men have died trying to free him…"

Stewart nodded as he pulled Bentuwi to his feet. "We'll see," he replied and pushed the man ahead of them into the cover of the sago. "All these African fuckers have a price…"

"I don't have a price, my friend," the Ugandan said pointedly. "I have beliefs. And I believe that a stable Africa can only be achieved when we put down the gun and respect one another."

Stewart pulled the man by his collar as he followed King. He would have glanced back at Paddy's body, but he had learned long ago never to look back. A soldier who had experienced battle never did. King held back as they dropped down a particularly high terrace, and between them they kept Bentuwi on the move. Years of limited physical activity and a poor, insufficient diet had taken their toll on the man, leaving him frail, and his joints and muscles noticeably stiff. Each descent down the metre-high terraces proved a considerable challenge for the man, his movements slow and laboured as he struggled to keep up. However, once they cleared the terraces and reached the slopes planted with maize, the going became markedly easier. The ground levelled out, making progress less taxing for him, and the head-high maize offered much-needed concealment, shielding them from view as they pressed forwards. Celebration was short lived as gunfire rained down around them, and King turned to see that the soldiers had finally regained their composure and were firing from the ridge some two hundred metres above them. King suspected that the elevation, distance and arc of bullet travel made the shots more difficult than the soldiers imagined, and clumps of soft earth spewed harmlessly into the air twenty feet from them, with the soldiers lacking the training and discipline to fine tune their shots closer to their target.

They reached the jungle after threading their way through the maize plantation, and Bentuwi was heaving for breath and becoming a deadweight as he increasingly tried to pause for breath, or slump to the ground to rest. Stewart dragged the man into the undergrowth and King kicked him unceremoniously up his backside in frustration to keep him moving.

Bentuwi went down hard, and King heaved him back up, but realised at once that something was wrong, and felt a pang of regret at kicking him when he saw the blood seeping through the man's trousers at his hip. "He's hit!" King shouted to Stewart.

"Fuck!" Stewart raged and pulled Bentuwi around like a carcass of meat to assess the damage. "Bollocks..."

"Sorry to disappoint you so..." Bentuwi commented, his tone sardonic.

"You really are a hard sell," said King as he tore at the man's shirt and wrapped it tightly around his groin and thigh to staunch the bleeding. "We're getting you out so that you can gain public support and remove President Museveni from office!"

Moffusa Bentuwi winced at the pain, shaking his head. "You seek to control Uganda and her resources through installing a figurehead. A puppet leader." He winced in pain. "It is the British way, even so long after the Empire has fallen. You still have not seen the error in this, or sought to change…"

Gunfire erupted suddenly to their right, echoing through the dense undergrowth. Bullets whistled dangerously close, tearing through leaves and branches or ricocheting off thick limbs overhead. Instinctively, King dropped to a knee and returned fire, his shots precise and deliberate. Two figures emerged from the brush, weapons raised, but they crumpled to the ground almost immediately under King's barrage. Without pause, King continued to fire, laying down suppressive fire as Stewart hauled Bentuwi forwards, urging him through the tangled foliage with force. Sensing movement deeper among the trees, King didn't hesitate; he yanked the pin from a fragmentation grenade and hurled it towards the shifting shadows. The explosion ripped through the jungle, sending a shockwave of noise and debris in all directions. He fired again, aiming at points a metre or more apart until the weapon clicked empty, and he hastily changed magazines before taking to his feet through the dense undergrowth. When he caught up with them, parts of a trauma kit was spilled out onto the ground and Stewart was pressing a wad of gauze into Bentuwi's side, looking back at King with a look that said many things, but most of all anger and disappointment. The man had been shot a second time, and this injury looked far more urgent than the wound to his hip.

King looked at the man with little compassion. If fate or

physics dictated that sooner or later bullets had to find someone, then he'd rather they found the Ugandan than Stewart or himself. His concern right now wasn't the fact that the mission had gone to shit, but getting out alive, and for that he knew that he needed to change the narrative and with it, the dynamic of the fight. He checked his watch, then said to Stewart, "You take him on ahead, I'll stay behind and give them something to think about..."

"King, we..."

"If we don't change this, then we'll all be killed." He tucked the rifle underneath his left armpit and proceeded to load one of the empty magazines with bullets from the cardboard carton that he had taken from the arms store. "You know I'm right..."

Stewart nodded, leaving Bentuwi to keep pressure on the gauze as he wrapped tape around the man's waist. When he had finished, he changed magazines and handed King his last two. "Hopefully you'll need these more than I will. I'll hold the chopper..."

"Will you fuck..." King shrugged. He knew how Stewart rolled when a mission was at stake. The man only ever saw the objective, not the personal cost.

Stewart shrugged. "Well, it sounded good, at least." He pulled Bentuwi to his feet and hoisted the man into a fireman's lift over his shoulder and bounced him about, despite the man's objections, until he had him well-balanced. He adjusted his grip on the heavy rifle. "Just don't be late," he added, then took off without looking back.

## Chapter Thirty-Six

King had skirted around leaving the discarded trauma kit as bait. He had wedged a fragmentation grenade underneath it and eased out the pin. He found a good place to lay up and wait and rested two spare magazines beside the rifle to his left for quick reloads, because like the British soldiers at Rorke's Drift, he wasn't going anywhere. He positioned two grenades to his right and then tore a strip off his shirt and wrapped it around the muzzle of the rifle to eliminate the muzzle flash – at least for the first half a dozen crucial shots. With just time and distance between life and death, King took a deep breath to steady his nerves.

The first to appear was a tentative soldier who stepped through the thick cover, his gaze restless and alert, scanning every shadow and flicker of movement. He cradled his AK47 tightly against his chest, gripping it as though it were both a lifeline and a deathly chalice, an object that could offer him survival just as easily as it could seal his fate. Each cautious step betrayed his anxiety, the tension evident in the way he hunched his shoulders and moved with measured, deliberate caution, all senses straining for any sign of threat in the oppressive jungle silence. The man was young – no older than sixteen, and King cursed silently. Soldiers hadn't been given the name *infantry* for nothing, and leaders had sent their youth to die for them for millennia. King waited, as a hunter would wait for more of the herd to follow, and sure enough two more stepped into the killing ground. By the time the boy had reached the abandoned trauma pack, six men stood before him. Only the oldest went to say something as the boy lifted the back and the spoon flicked high into the air arming the grenade's five second fuse. King fired after two seconds had passed, just to add to the chaos and indecision. The grenade detonated without Hollywood flames or catapulting bodies, but when the smoke and debris cleared, the boy and another soldier were on the ground in crumpled, unmoving heaps. King fired and cut down the rest of the men as they fired wildly off target. He changed magazines and tossed one of the grenades into the undergrowth towards where he caught some movement. The grenade detonated with a thump which he felt through the ground, and he heard screams as at least two men were struck by shrapnel. Gunfire erupted to his left, and he pivoted on the ground to meet two men charging head-on towards him. Bullets streaked the ground in front of him, and he fired most of the magazine to take down both attackers. King picked up the other grenade and lobbed it in the direction that they had come from and rolled back to pick up the second magazine and reload. He now had a few magazines with an indeterminable quantity of ammunition remaining and needed to have some time to replenish and square away, but that was a luxury that he did not have, and he sprung to his feet and charged through the undergrowth towards the enemy rather than fleeing. Some problems in life could only be met head on.

King met two men almost at once, and he drove the muzzle of the rifle into the man's stomach as if it were a bayonet charge, and only then noticed that the cloth had been blown apart and what little remained was scorched and in tatters. The second man took the butt of the rifle to the face, and rather than waist precious ammunition for the rifle at close quarters, King drew the pistol as he regained his balance and shot both men once each through the head as they writhed on the ground. He was met with gunfire at once, and he dropped to the ground using one of the bodies for cover as he aimed the rifle towards the muzzle flashes and returned fire. It was close quarters now, men pushing their way through the brush, just feet in front of King, and finding themselves in the seven circles of hell. King operated on automatic pilot. He fired, reloaded, switched to his pistol, charged, dodged, used his knife when his rifle clicked empty, and picked up weapons, ditching them just as quickly when they clicked empty. There was no plan, no body count, merely kill or be killed. When the area finally fell silent, King did not hesitate. He snatched up a weapon and ran. His escape, however, was short lived, and he dived for cover as the jungle behind him erupted in gunfire from another direction. As far as he could make out, he was all but cut off with just a slim route of escape. He did not know which way that headed, but he was taking it at any cost. Risking being funnelled into his enemy's killing ground, he charged through the brush and straight into three men who looked both stunned and confused. Their enemy had moved too soon, and the surprise and annoyance showed on their faces as King fired. When all three men were dead or dying on the ground, King only then realised that he had ditched the rifle mid-contact and was holding the pistol. Stewart's training had almost become part of his DNA. There had been no thought, merely action.

There was movement in the jungle behind him, and King picked up a spare magazine for the rifle before dragging one of the bodies by its ankle and dropping it in front of another body, before laying down behind his makeshift barrier.

King reached for another magazine on the corpse in front of him, tugging it out from the man's otherwise depleted bandolier. He wasn't certain if the bodies would afford him protection from enemy bullets, but they did at least shield him from view and provide the rifle with a steady rest. He needed to make every shot count, and it was imperative that he dropped the first soldiers who stepped out from cover because watching your comrades fall quickly usually got a man's attention. Behind him, if Stewart was still alive, and still carried Moffusa Bentuwi on his back like a sack of maize through the jungle, then he was their ticket out of here. No Bentuwi, no ride home. The pilot would wait for the country's legitimate choice for presidential successor, but he would be wheels up at first sight of two white mercenaries staggering out of the jungle alone, let alone with half the Ugandan army in pursuit. The pilot had already been paid half his fee to get Bentuwi out and he would not get the other half of his fee without him, and he wouldn't give a damn about just King and Stewart, who would be more trouble than it was worth.

The first man through the brush was barely a man. King did not want to think about his age, because an AK47 was as dangerous in a boy's hands as in anybody else's. His eyes were keen, but that keenness was derived only through fear. He stepped over the body of one of his comrades, his eyes everywhere at once. Another soldier stepped into the clearing, older, wiser. He had allowed the boy to go first. There was no love lost in battle.

King checked his watch, mentally doing the maths. It was three miles to the extraction point, and he had thirty-two minutes to do it. Stewart might manage to convince the pilot to wait at the business end of a gun, but even then, the tough Scotsman would have his own deadline and if King did not meet it then it would be wheels up and out of there, and he knew that the bastard wouldn't lose a wink of sleep over it. Not now the mission had gone tits up, and they had lost control of a member of their team. Peter Stewart would be thinking of little more than damage limitation and cutting loose ends.

A third soldier entered the clearing, and then a fourth. That ought to be about right. More than that and if he had a weapon malfunction or took a bullet, then he would not be able to control the situation. He had seen firsthand what the Ugandan forces did to prisoners, and he had been left under no illusion that it would mean curtains if that happened.

King shot the boy between the eyes, then fired three shots centre mass at the second man. Two more double taps and the other two went down. He backed up into the brush as all hell broke out, and muzzle flashes lit the dull undergrowth like a hundred fireflies. He swapped to a new magazine, tucking the used one with twelve remaining rounds into his pocket for later. With a 7.62x51mm round already chambered, he had twenty-one shots remaining. Having taken just a few steps into the brush, he pulled the pin on a frag and tossed the grenade behind him into the clearing. There was no flame, no men catapulting into the air, but three of the enemy went down, fragmentation shrapnel cutting their legs, bodies and faces to pieces. The rest of the soldiers gave the clearing a wide berth, and as they skirted the treeline they wasted precious minutes while King sprinted full-pace through the undergrowth. Pulling the pin on a smoke grenade, he tossed it behind him and kept running. Behind him, orange smoke billowed in the wind, slowing his pursuers as they decided against running blindly into the dense, orange fog. King stopped and turned around, bracing the weapon against the trunk of a tree as he fired groups of three shots in a progressive arc until the weapon clicked empty. He reloaded, then tossed a fragmentation grenade high in the air and counted off five seconds, which was about the time it took to complete its arc and detonate the moment it hit the ground. He heard the solid thud, followed by screams, and he tossed the last of his smoke grenades into the trees, turned and sprinted through the undergrowth having significantly slowed their progress.

King checked his watch again. It was going to be close. Stewart was way ahead of him now, and he had the man that they had set out to free. Why would Stewart wait for him? He had what he came for, and because of one team member, civil war had broken out and genocide in neighbouring Rwanda was now a harsh, ugly reality. Questions would be asked, and Stewart wouldn't want any contradictions in his story. MI6 would batten down the hatches so anybody not singing from the same hymn sheet would be a problem. If Stewart took off with Moffusa Bentuwi, and King met his fate at the hands of the Ugandan army, then there would be nobody around to refute Stewart's 'truth'. Now that the thought had come to him, King could think of little else. There was no guarantee that even if he reached the extraction point in time, Stewart would hold the helicopter. Stewart could order the pilot to take off the moment he got there. Moffusa Bentuwi was the objective. Stewart wouldn't risk failure waiting for a junior operative with just three years' experience in the field. That wasn't something the Scotsman would risk his pension on. It wasn't even something the man would risk his next drink on. Stewart had lost Richard Collins, to lose King would set him back, but there were mouldable young men in the army, perhaps even in prison, that Stewart could train and shape for future missions. He'd done it before, and he'd do it again.

King checked his watch again. It would be tight, but he could do it. The distance with the time remaining would be challenging if he was wearing trainers and running kit, and as part of a nice, flat park run. In torn and soaked fatigues and wearing heavy boots and carrying twenty-pounds of kit and ammunition and a ten-pound loaded rifle, it was another matter entirely. The terrain was undulating, thick with brush and scattered with rocks, and strewn with sun-bleached carcasses that had sustained both land and fauna for millennia. He could do it. He knew he could. But what if he could not shake off the soldiers behind him? What if Stewart did not wait to the extraction zero hour? He would arrive in a state of exhaustion – he had already been on the go for forty-eight hours without rest – he would not be able to keep fighting and would surely be captured – and that would mean that he would become a political bargaining chip. MI6 would deny his very existence – as well they could, because of Stewart's secretive department with no links to the Secret Intelligence Service – and President Yoweri K. Museveni would not only be out for blood, but would parade King in front of the world's media to strengthen his support from the African Union, whose member states had been most critical of his tyrannical regime.

King stopped in his tracks, turned and knelt beside a

## Crossfire

large baobab tree, its thick trunk capable of stopping any bullet short of an anti-aircraft round. He pressed his stomach and chest into the soft bark, grateful for its protection, brought the weapon up to aim. He would have preferred it if the weapon had been fitted with a decent optic, but beggars couldn't be choosers. He had just killed a man for it, and up until then, he had engaged the enemy with just his 9mm Browning pistol after abandoning his rifle when he had run out of ammunition. King removed the bandolier that he had also relieved one of the dead men of and dropped it on the ground beside him. The bergen followed. All that he carried on his person now was a two-pint water bottle, his holstered pistol and sheath knife.

King steadied himself, eyes fixed on the dense undergrowth. He caught a flicker of movement among the trees and held his breath, waiting for confirmation. After a moment, three men materialised from the brush, their approach marked by an unnatural stillness. They moved cautiously, reminiscent of deer picking their way through the mist at dawn, alert to every sound and shadow. The tension in the air was palpable as King braced for what would come next, knowing that every decision in this moment could mean the difference between survival and death. He placed the iron sights on the first man, a post on the fore-end and a ringed aperture, or ghost ring, at the rear. He was aiming for centre mass. The spinal column was the goal, but if his aim was off that left the heart, aorta, and lungs. His finger tightened on the trigger, and taking a deep breath, he squeezed. The rifle leapt in his hands, the stock hammering into his shoulder, but he was already moving the sights to the second man and he fired again, and then at the third. All three men went down. Two of them resting still, the third man writhing on the ground and screaming.

King left the man alone. Not because he was feeling particularly merciful, but because the man may have friends who would attend to him, and in doing so, put more strain on the enemy force. He had one last fragmentation grenade, and he wedged it underneath his discarded bergen and pulled the pin. There was little point exhausting himself to make the extraction; wasn't even sure that Stewart would wait, anyway. He needed a Plan B. Something that would give him options if he did not make the extraction point in time, something he could switch to if he ended up a mile short and too exhausted to fight. Backing away from the wounded soldier and the sounds of men pressing onwards through the brush, King checked the compass hanging around his neck underneath his tattered shirt, soaked in both blood and sweat. Almost all of Uganda was to the north and he had burned his bridges there. The LRA thugs were to the west, and killing everyone who stood in their way, and Rwanda had broken into civil war to the south. Which left Tanzania to the east. Jakaya Kikwete had just won a landslide election with eighty per cent of the vote, and the country was in jubilant spirits. The army was pressing west to secure the border with Rwanda succumbing to genocide, and if the Tutsis were overrun, then a mass migration crisis would see the border flooded with war refugees. If he could get through, he had a contact in the press who was covering the election victory, and something to do with orphanages losing government funding. King did not have friends, but he considered his press contact, a former lover, would be as close to a friend as he had. It was certainly worth a try.

# Chapter Thirty-Seven
## Nyarugusu Aid Camp, Northwest Tanzania

King nursed his cup of tea and stared at the sunset. He shifted on the dry earth, his legs aching, his body tired. A nurse from the Red Cross tent had washed and patched his grazes, stitched his cuts. Stewart was still having treatment for the bullet graze, that trivialised the deep gash made in his leg when his initial assault had been compromised. King reflected that the man was a tough old bastard, and he was sure that he did not want to be in this line of work when he was in his forties.

King had made it to the extraction point, and the helicopter pilot had taken off not knowing that Moffusa Bentuwi had succumbed to his injuries. Stewart had propped the would-be-should-have-been President of Uganda in the seat against the bulkhead and given the man further medical attention, but when the man had passed away, he had continued to maintain the charade and wait for King. Once they had taken off, they had been given a bird's eye view of the pursuing Ugandan forces and a group of LRA rebels who had heard the gunfire and advanced to intercept disrupters of the Lord's work. It had been a close thing, and King had closed his eyes and relished the ride to safety. They had headed east flying low over the border, as arranged with MI6's government contact who had paid off air traffic control, and the pilot had taken them to the nearby aid camp, not knowing that Moffusa Bentuwi was dead until they were on the ground with the rotors winding down.

King sipped some more of his tea. Four comrades dead, Ginnie slain in their room for nothing more than to hurt King, and countless Ugandans killed, and for what? No purpose whatsoever. No further forward on whatever board the men and women in government and MI6 played on. The counter reset to start, like an immersive game of Snakes and Ladders.

"You look like hell..."

King looked up, the woman's face shaded by the sunset behind her, but he recognised the voice and his heart suddenly raced. "Lucinda..." he said, getting painfully to his feet. She lunged at him; her arms wrapped around him in something far greater than that of two former lovers wanting to rekindle. She sobbed and he could feel her heart pounding through her breast pushed firmly against his chest. "My God, what's wrong?"

"Hold me, don't let me go..."

King held her firmly in his arms. He was sure that he loved her, but their story was a complicated one. She was married and had married well. He couldn't give her anything but his raw personality and animalistic sex. Her husband was a member of the cabinet, and she was climbing the ladder in media, from a columnist to correspondent, to a television journalist. King was a killer working for a secretive department within MI6. Their relationship was a nonstarter. Stewart had made that much clear. "I'm here," he comforted her.

She did not speak for a good five minutes, but King did not find it uncomfortable. He was giving her what she had asked for, what she needed. Eventually, she said, "It was so horrible..."

"You don't have to say a thing," he told her. "I'm here for you..."

She sobbed into his chest, her body slack as he took her weight and she relaxed into him. "I held a baby in my arms..." she said quietly. "...and he killed..." She hesitated, still unsure whether the poor child had been a boy or a girl. All she could think about was how the poor child's head had blown apart, how she had felt the warmth of the wet splatter on her face. "He killed the baby..." she sobbed. "Then they cut off my cameraman's and editor's arms..."

"Jesus Christ..." King said quietly, wishing he could have been more loquacious under the circumstances, but he had never used five words when one would do.

"Then..."

King already knew. She was standing there, her arms clinging to him as if her life depended on it, and it was obvious to him that, although everyone in their group had suffered, Lucinda's experience had been something altogether different. The sort of people capable of severing a man's arm for their own amusement would never simply let a woman go free—least of all a strikingly beautiful woman like Lucinda Davenport. He held her tightly, understanding that her pain ran deeper than any words could express. The horrors she had witnessed were etched in her trembling embrace and the haunted look in her eyes. King's own wounds, which had stung and ached and throbbed as he had relaxed and sipped his tea were now forgotten. Paled in comparison to what she had endured, and he was painfully aware that survival for Lucinda had come at a terrible cost. The violence inflicted upon her colleagues, and the trauma she carried, were reminders of the brutal reality they all faced. In that moment, King resolved to be her anchor, to offer solace against the darkness that threatened to consume her. He thought back to the first time he had set eyes on her on a swimming pool terrace in Angola before embarking into the DRC. She had captivated him as she had lain in her bikini in the sun, and she had intrigued him with her passion for reporting the truth. He was from a different world, and he had never been in the company of such a woman, who had challenged him and filled him with admiration. That woman now seemed a shell of her former self, and he would do whatever he could to bring her back.

"How are they doing?" he asked. "Your cameraman and editor…" He closed his eyes, regretting asking such an inane question. How the hell did he think they were doing?

Despite his asinine question she said quietly, "I don't think they can quite take it in, now that they have been sedated. Strangely, they're more grateful to be alive than mourning the loss of a limb. But once they have surgery in a few hours and come round, I suspect the full horror will dawn on them," she sighed heavily. "What a crazy, cruel world we live in…"

King knew that to be true, and he wondered whether his work deterred or created such cruelness. "Where are they now?" he asked, to keep her talking and her mind off whatever hell she had suffered.

"In there, with your boss," she replied. "I saw him being wheeled into the triage. The old coot saw me, too. My God, I hate that man…"

"Sometimes, I do, too," King replied.

## Crossfire

She hugged him tightly again, then slowly pulled away and looked up into his eyes blinking through tears and the rawness of crying. "They were animals," she said, her mind still there and her tone distant enough to be there, too. "I have had to be tested for HIV and God only knows what else. He really damaged me, too. I don't think I'll ever be able to tell my husband..."

King was lost for words. Although he knew who her husband was, he had always tried to ignore the man's existence. "He loves you," he said eventually. "So, he'll understand and he will be there for you."

"He's cheating on me," she replied, then shrugged. "But I cheated on him with you several times, so we're both as messed up as the other. Our marriage is a sham, and this is when I'm going to need him the most..."

King held her comfortingly, and it dawned on him that he had never previously been there for somebody. He was there for a person, not hoping to get something out of the situation, not taking advantage of her vulnerability, but *actually* wanting to help. "It may be a moment of make or break for you both," he replied eventually, when the silence became palpable. "Perhaps being there for you will make you both realise what's important." He shrugged. "Maybe you just both lost your way, and from now on, you will both see what is important, and what really matters."

Lucinda sighed. "Relationship advice from the only man I think I've ever truly loved..."

"Who did this to you, Lucinda?" King asked.

She linked her arm in his and started to walk. It was obviously painful for her and King thought it was just so she did not have to look at him. "He called himself Colonel Jones..." she replied, then shrugged. "Doesn't sound very Rwandan, does it? He'll never be found, anyway. Not in that hell-hole. Who the hell is going to care about one solitary rape? Of a Westerner, no less. There will have been tens of thousands, if not hundreds of thousands of rapes. They have weaponised the brutality of the act, as sure as if they had pulled a trigger."

King nodded. But there were other ways to get justice. "Rwandans don't have generic surnames as we do in the West," he told her. "Instead, like Ugandans and the Burindis, they have clan names, of which there are around fifty, or they have a name given after an achievement of event. The clan names are Rwandan words for monkey, lion, elephant, hippo and other animals. I think if he was serious about his name being Jones, then something quintessentially British could be a link."

"Really?"

King nodded and led her onwards. He was grateful to keep moving, just for the fact that he did not want her to see the sadness and pity in his eyes. "I will find out," he said eventually. "I'm wondering whether a Colonel who has adopted a thoroughly British name did so because he did his officer training at Sandhurst, and that was considered an achievement within his family or clan. Rwandans don't just stick to their given clan names but rather wait for a defining moment in their lives."

"How would you find out?" she asked hopefully.

King thumbed back at the cluster of Red Cross hospital tents and said, "That *old coot* in there having his leg sewn up would be my guess. And I have a few contacts who can search MOD files if he won't play ball."

"Secretaries and PAs at the River House, who swoon over you like James Bond?" she scoffed.

King smiled, pleased to see her resilience kicking in. A woman like Lucinda Davenport could be knocked down, but she would always get back up again. "I doubt they've ever swooned," he replied. "But some of them have put aside a larger mug for me if tea gets served..."

"Thanks. But it won't do any good. The country is in chaos," she said somewhat distantly. "What's just another rape and two Western journalists maimed in the scheme of what's happening over there? Even the murder of a baby will pale into insignificance in the wake of such wholesale slaughter." She shook her head. "How will life ever be the same again? How will I move on knowing that a man is out there having done this to me?" She shrugged, wiping a tear from her cheek. "I know that must sound selfish, given the state of my colleagues and the murder of that beautiful little baby, but I can't ever imagine moving past this..."

King shook his head. No, he couldn't imagine her moving past this. But he certainly knew how to make a start.

# Chapter Thirty-Eight

"You're fucking kidding me..." Stewart shook his head. "You've gone soft in the head, lad."

"It's just an email," King persisted. "You send one, you get one back."

"No."

"It's all I'm asking."

"Still no..."

"Then I'll find another way," King said as he caught hold of the curtain. "I'll see you, when I see you..."

"Wait!" Stewart snapped, rolling his eyes as he swung both feet painfully over the edge of the bed. His right leg was heavily bandaged. Not for the bullet graze, but for the infection that had set in and since been cut away and packed with wadding soaked in iodine. He had been told to rest for a week before flying because of the risk of swelling, and the Red Cross surgeon had arranged for Stewart's dressing to be changed and monitored at a hospital in the capital, before being stitched. "What good will it do?"

King shrugged. "It needs to be done."

"We need to fly back to London in a week," he said

adamantly. "And when we get there, there'll be a shit-storm waiting. It might well be it for me, and by association, that may well mean you too."

King pulled the curtain back and said, "Then do this one thing for me..."

## Chapter Thirty-Nine
### Rwanda

"I can't do this."

"Yes, you can."

"I'm scared!"

"I know."

"Please, Alex," Lucinda said quietly.

King could not get used to his name. It just never felt right when someone called him Alex. For him, he was always Mark. He could handle the surname, but the first name never seemed right, and he always introduced himself as King to save the charade. Lucinda had wanted to know the first name of the man she was sleeping with back in Angola, so he had naturally obliged. "I get it," he said gently. "But trust me, you'll sleep better in five years' time knowing you did this..."

"Why? Why are you helping me?"

King shrugged but said nothing. The truth was simple, even if he rarely admitted it out loud: he loved her. That much he knew, deep within himself. But the situation was far more complex than just his own feelings. He also understood that Lucinda loved her husband. Their relationship was tangled—at times complicated, at others outright toxic. King recognised there was no real future for the two of them; there could be no sweeping Lucinda away from her marriage, no possibility of a clean break or a happy ending. The painful reality was that she was both a cause and a victim of the problems within her relationship. Some people, King reflected, were simply destined to be together—even if that meant enduring a life that was more miserable than joyful.

They had travelled through Rwanda using Lucinda's press pass and that of Ian Gallagher, who bore a passing resemblance to King. King had familiarised himself with the man's camera and lighting equipment and had stowed his pistol and ammunition inside the case, and a lot more besides, taking it out and making the weapon ready the moment they crossed over into the war-torn country via a circuitous mountain route of tracks and offroad, avoiding the border crossing, but always against a swathe of refugees fleeing the horrors of war. King didn't have much of a plan, other than they would head back to the scene of the crime, and Stewart had begrudgingly sent for information on the Colonel, who as King suspected had completed his officer training at Sandhurst. Rwanda had applied to join the British Commonwealth at a time when many of the Caribbean nations were seeking to leave, with its membership pending. King knew that 'Great Britain PLC' was in the business of military industries and officer training was a major income stream for the British economy. However, the man had been sent down for cheating and was only in his role in the Rwandan military because of well-placed family members. He was in fact called Jones, taking the name when he was accepted into officer training. His given name was Rukundo, meaning love. An irony that was not lost on Lucinda.

Stewart's analyst contact had said that Rwanda had quickly been divided into sectors, with each sector assigned a major or colonel and a battalion of men. If they wanted to find Colonel 'Rukundo' Jones, then if he had held onto his sector, then that's where the man would be.

On the second day they had come across two nuns and twenty children, and Lucinda had told the sisters about the orphanage in Tanzania and written a letter of introduction for them to show the orphanage chaplain. If she couldn't cover the story, then she would at least help the children, the casualties of war.

On the third day, they had followed the smoke, and as they had drawn closer, the smell of burning flesh. King thought it smelled like burnt roasting pork, and by the time they reached the first of the funeral pyres, he had vowed never to eat roast pork again. The thought alone making him feel sick to his stomach. There were dozens of piles of bodies, the fires all started with tyres and wood and anything else that could be found that was flammable. It was clear that once the pyres had burned fiercely, the rendering fat was continuously fuelling the flames, the fires hissing and flaring and spitting – almost breathing - a living, malevolent entity of destructive heat and flame.

All around them, people were steadily making their way towards the border, driven by fear and desperation. King watched the crowds, his thoughts turning to the inevitable consequences: this movement would undoubtedly escalate into a full-blown migrant crisis. He could already picture what would happen once those fleeing realised that, for many, Europe represented the only real hope of safety. Britain, in particular, would become the most accessible destination for countless refugees. Commentators would argue that once out of Rwanda, the refugees would be safe. And yet, King could not help but question the logic of that argument. What rational person would willingly abandon their home only to seek refuge in a country that could prove just as hostile as the one they had left behind? Of course they would head to Europe and within Europe, Britain would always be the beacon of hope.

He found himself contemplating the true extent of Richard Collins' impact on the world. When Collins had fired the rocket launcher, could he have possibly foreseen the far-reaching consequences of that single act? King imagined the event as a stone cast into a still lake, the resulting ripples spreading outward in every direction. The consequences, once set in motion, would continue to reverberate, touching countless lives and situations, only coming to an eventual halt when the surrounding circumstances finally brought them to rest.

After they had driven for another three hours Lucinda finally said somewhat sombrely, "This is it..."

King nodded and pulled the hired Nissan Patrol 4x4 to the side of the road. He said nothing as Lucinda sat and stared at the hut, and he figured that was where the unspeakable act had happened, and he knew that it was too soon – if ever there could be such a time – for Lucinda to be back here, and without King having anything more than the bare bones of a plan and the luck of a gambler at the roulette table who had just put everything including his shirt on 00. As he looked at the dying embers of a funeral pyre, wondering whether both mother and baby had been eradicated and turned to ash to blow onto the plains. Never was there a continent where 'the circle of life' played out so purely as a coined phrase as in Africa.

Here, the inevitability of life and death was ever-present, revealed in the daily struggle for survival and the stark realities faced by its people. The balance between creation and destruction, hope and despair, was laid bare for all to see. In Africa, the cycles of existence—birth, growth, decay and renewal—were not merely abstract notions but visceral truths, experienced in the land itself and in the lives of those who called it home. The phrase 'circle of life' took on a raw, unfiltered meaning in this place, echoing through every act of nature and human endeavour alike.

"I'm sorry," he said, staring at the dying embers of the pyre, the finality of people's lives, their story erased and left untold. "This wasn't a good idea. We should go."

Lucinda sighed. "I get why we're doing this," she replied. "But you're right. We *should* go. My job is to tell peoples' stories. I can do good by reporting what has happened here..." She smiled, briefly distracted from the trauma. "What were you going to do? Take on a dozen men with a handgun?" She paused. "Let's go. Thank you for trying, but I think I want to go home now."

King reached out and placed a hand comfortingly on her knee hoping to convey both reassurance and understanding. He knew that by going home, she meant to her husband, and the strangest sensation came over him as he didn't mind at all. He just wanted her to be happy, and if that was what it took, then so be it. He started the engine, instinctively checking his mirrors, then hesitated. "Bugger..." he said quietly.

Lucinda spun around in her seat. "Oh, God no..."

The pickup truck rolled in behind them and King dragged the camera bag off the back seat and rested it in his lap. "Stay calm, and when I move, hit the ground, cover your ears and stay there..." He pulled the bag with him and opened his door.

"Alex, no..." Lucinda grabbed his arm, but he pulled away, catching the look of terror, the desperation in her eyes. "I love you..." she managed to say, the words leaving in the merest croak through her dry lips.

"Get out!" one of the men shouted as he leapt out of the truck carrying a Kalashnikov and alternating his aim between King and the vehicle.

Lucinda opened her door slowly and climbed down. When she dared to look, King was standing with his left arm raised, and the bag in his right hand. He was saying something to the soldier, but she could not hear past the pumping of blood in her ears, the sound of her own breathing seemingly drowning out all other noise. She raised her trembling hands, then felt her heart almost explode as the Colonel stepped out of the passenger side, cleaning his mirrored aviators on his shirt. Her legs buckled, and she dropped to the dusty, ash-covered earth as she locked eyes on her rapist.

"You...?" Colonel Jones said, unable to hide his surprise. He turned to King as he neared and said, "You know what was done to this whore's colleagues?"

"Of course," King replied. "That's why we're here..."

"You want to lose an arm?"

"No."

"We shall see," the Colonel replied, almost drunk on power, such was his confidence. "Then she must have returned for more cock, then."

"No."

"Then what?" the man asked somewhat dubiously. "To write a story? To film me?"

"No."

"I don't understand."

"I don't expect you to." King glanced at the pickup truck. There was a driver and five men in the back with one of them manning the .50 machinegun, but he was looking bored. King figured the man had seen this sight a dozen times before. The soldier standing close to the colonel, unsure where to aim his weapon was looking more relaxed than he previously had, and he was sneering at Lucinda sitting sobbing on the ground.

"Then why are you here?"

King shrugged. "To kill you..."

The colonel frowned as King pulled on a length of paracord and tossed the bag towards the pickup truck. He drew the pistol and shot the soldier beside him through the forehead before the bag landed on the bonnet of the truck. Colonel Jones just had time to recognise the eight ring-pins from the grenades hanging from the length of cord in King's hand before he shot the man in his right eye. King dived for Lucinda and covered her as the .50 fired, tearing up the ground where he had been standing, but the weapon was drowned out as the grenades exploded in unison, blowing out the windscreen and vaporising the driver and spreading deadly shrapnel into the bed of the pickup. King rolled away from Lucinda and scrambled to his feet. He sprinted hard for the truck and fired at anything that moved. It was over in less than six seconds, and he had fired a dozen rounds in all. As he walked back to Lucinda, who was getting slowly to her feet, he shot the colonel twice more in his head then tossed the empty pistol onto the ground and picked up the dead soldier's AK47.

"Are you okay?" he asked as he flicked the weapon to 'safe'.

## Crossfire

"Yes..." she replied quietly, numb from shock and relief. "Then let's get out of here..."

# Chapter Forty
## London

An interview without coffee. Stewart knew the significance, had even heard the term thrown into gossip and derogative conversation around the offices and corridors of the River House and at Century House before SIS had relocated a decade before. The last time he had had an interview without coffee he had spent the next year seconded to MI5 in their Airports and Ports division, watching travellers through two-way mirrors and checking against watch lists and police bulletins. He had been a glorified customs officer and had turned to drink, had three affairs, and almost died from boredom.

So, here he was again at 85, Albert Embankment in Vauxhall, London, in what MI6 across the river called The Lego House, seated in a dull, twenty by twenty room without windows or so much as a single framed hotel print on the walls. Even the furniture was Formica and steel and straight out of an underfunded comprehensive school. To add insult to injury, Stewart had ended a few careers in a room very much like this one. You reaped what you sowed in this life. He had had his doubts about

## Crossfire

Richard Collins, and had ignored his instructors and directing staff, his gut instinct, and even King's opinion because he had seen something raw, something untrainable in the man. And now it had come to bite him in the arse.

The door opened and two mandarins walked in without looking at him. Both carried a briefcase and a cup of tea or coffee on a saucer. *So, it was like that*, thought Stewart. But Stewart had been around the block and had been spying, deceiving, killing, and running foreign assets before these two sociology graduates had thought about their GCSE options.

Samantha Long spoke first. "Rwanda is on you, Mr Stewart. Thoughts?"

"It's a bloody massacre," Roland Brown interjected. "Over a million slaughtered, government forces struggling to hold ground, rebels and warring factions vying for control, it's a bloody nightmare!"

"Richard Collins was profiled and interviewed regularly, his psych-reports were satisfactory, considering you're talking about a trained killer, and nobody saw what was coming." Stewart stared at them both but offered nothing more.

"Where is he?"

"It's fluid. I have an agent on the ground, and he is making good progress."

"And what are your agent's orders?" Roland Brown asked, his tone churlish.

"To terminate."

"With extreme prejudice?" Samantha Long asked, raising an eyebrow. "Rather an unusual order for an agent to be given without the proper chain of command or going through the necessary channels.

"Termination is only ever with extreme prejudice," Stewart commented flatly.

"Nevertheless, you are not in a position to give such an order."

Stewart looked at the woman. Early thirties, unmarried – a career mandarin, and she had done well to get so many rungs up the ladder in such a short time. "Lady, I make decisions like this every day. It's why I exist. So that people like you don't get your pretty, little hands dirty..."

"There's no need to get snippy, Mr Stewart," Brown sneered somewhat disdainfully. "And this agent of yours, it's Alex King, isn't it?"

"Yes."

"The man who lost the money and safecracker in France?"

Stewart shrugged. "Who also exposed and killed a rogue agent..."

"Who cocked up in Beirut?" Samantha Long smirked.

"Beirut is a difficult place to operate. My agents made it out alive. That's a win."

"But your asset did not..." Brown said mockingly, a supercilious grin on his plump lips. "A man holding great sway and with a unique position within Hamas. That sounds very much like a loss, to me."

Stewart, who seemed quite unfazed, and ignoring them both, said, "Talking of dirty hands..." He stared coldly at Brown. Like Samantha Long, the man was in his early thirties, but he was married with an eight-month-old, and it showed around his eye sockets. "That was a rather messy affair in Brussels. It all got resolved, though, didn't it?" Stewart stared at him, enjoying the flicker of resignation and doubt, then fear in his tired-looking eyes.

"What is he talking about, Roland?"

"Nothing."

"It doesn't sound like nothing…"

"It's nothing!" Roland Brown snapped, instantly regretting it. He was many things, but a poker player wasn't one of them.

"Yes. Nothing," Stewart smiled. "Messy enough to cost you your job and marriage, but all sorted. A bit like those two young girls from Birmingham who ran off to join al-Qaeda. That's something you know about, isn't it, Ms Long?"

"What is he talking about, Samantha?" Roland turned to her curiously, but the man certainly had an inkling.

Two fifteen-year-old girls had fallen in love with the ideology of Islamic fundamentalism and had not turned up for school one Monday morning in November, four years previously. CCTV tracked them taking a train from Birmingham New Street to London Marylebone Station, and the underground to Paddington Station and the direct line to Heathrow Airport. From there, they had flown to Islamabad. Their bodies had been discovered in the Helmand Province of Afghanistan three years later by US Marines after an airstrike. The two girls had been married off several times over - each time their al-Qaeda husbands had been killed - and had perished alongside their seven children. There had been unsubstantiated accusations from the girls' parents that their daughters had been played by the British security services, initially recruited by an undercover MI6 or MI5 officer posing as an Islamic extremist. It had never been proven, but Peter Stewart had a file in his safekeeping, and Samantha Long's name appeared in it. Stewart had made it his business to keep files on the people who could take him down or hang him out to dry. He called it his 'security blanket' and it helped him sleep at night. He held files on almost all the top pen-pushers in MI6, and it never ceased to amaze him how people messed up in life. There were career mistakes, bad debts, affairs – Stewart wasn't fussy what went into the files, so long as it could be used against them. Famously, J. Edgar Hoover, one of the instrumental men behind the founding of the FBI, and the bureau's first director had kept files on anyone of influence, be it political or business, or even Hollywood – anything that would make his job easier and provide him with leverage. Stewart had merely learnt from one of the grand masters of espionage and law enforcement.

"Well, this is awkward," Stewart smiled, still leaning confidently back in his chair with the look of a man who had four aces and did not hide the fact behind a poker face. He eyed them both in turn, then said, "Would you care to take turns stepping outside, or should we air all our dirty linen publicly?"

"I don't think..." Brown trailed off, his face flushed and perspiration on his brow.

Stewart stared at Long, who shook her head and looked away. "Right. Here's how it's going to play out. My agent is hunting down Richard Collins and will take the man out of the picture. The blame for Rwanda will ultimately come down to rebels and tribes settling old scores, and the inevitability of living inside a social powder keg. As we say so often, TIA. This Is Africa. It is an old and familiar story, and I doubt we will ever live to see the last of it." He paused, standing up and wincing as the stitches in his leg pulled. He had undergone a lot of cutting to remove the infection and had needed the wounds restitched after landing at Heathrow. The chair toppled over and he ignored it, having no intention of returning it to the table. "The civil war in Rwanda will end. And when it does,

**Crossfire**

Britian will undoubtedly be first in the queue to plunder her resources, strike up new deals and offer thoughts and prayers to those affected. Bob Geldof will write another song, and Lenny Henry will spend another night on Comic Relief attempting to inject humour into a melancholy backdrop of awkward television, leaving the viewers wondering if he was ever funny in the first place..."

## Chapter Forty-One
### Cape Town South Africa

Clifton was a beachside town renowned for its luxurious properties, rivalling those found in Malibu or Santa Monica, yet available at only a fraction of the price. Known as the Jewel in the Cape, the town was distinguished by its pristine, sugar-white beaches, dotted with immense, smooth boulders that sheltered the shoreline from the relentless crash of Atlantic waves. The region experienced dramatic seasonal contrasts, with the waters turning cold during winter months and warming in the summer, inviting both locals and tourists alike.

King and Lucinda had returned to Tanzania and by the time they reached the Red Cross station, Peter Stewart had left for the hospital in the capital. When King checked with the hospital administration, he had been informed that Stewart had discharged himself and taken a taxi to the airport. King had remained in the camp while Lucinda had checked on Ian and Malcolm, and she had arranged via her satellite news channel that they be taken by private ambulance to a private hospital in the capital. King and Lucinda had booked into a hotel near the hospital in separate rooms

## Crossfire

and had enjoyed a dinner and drinks together, with King escorting her to her room. He had checked the room for her like one would a small child suffering from disturbed sleep and nightmares – checking the wardrobe, under the bed and in the bathroom, before waiting outside while she had fixed the chain and locked the door. Lucinda was due to fly out for Heathrow the next day, and when King had called upon her for breakfast, he found that she had checked out. No note, no message. King knew what that meant, and he wished her well and hoped that one day, their paths would cross again.

King looked down on the white sands of the beaches. He had driven the route yesterday, marvelling at the somewhat familiar scenery that bore more than a fleeting resemblance of Exmoor or the Scottish Highlands, but along with deer and buffalo, ostriches scratched and pecked the ground in search of food, while troops of baboons scavenged along the roadside. On the white sands below, penguins competed for space with beachgoers, their comical waddling providing a unique spectacle, while just offshore, great white sharks cruised through the waters, with the blowhole spray of breaching whales far offshore. Clifton's blend of natural beauty, fascinating wildlife, and striking coastal scenery made it a truly distinctive destination. These distinctive sights served as a constant reminder that, for all its familiar scenery, visitors were unmistakably in South Africa. The juxtaposition of rolling hills and indigenous wildlife created a sense of place unlike any other, blending the comfort of recognisable terrain with the thrill of encountering exotic creatures in their natural habitat. King thought the country to be the most unique and fascinating place he had ever been.

King pulled over to the side of the road and parked his

vehicle. He had chosen a white Toyota Corolla, a model that was as inconspicuous and unremarkable as they come. The decision had been made with deliberate care for two reasons; at the Hertz rental car park at the airport, there had been a row of twenty identical cars, each blending seamlessly into the next. With such a common choice, King felt reassured that he would not draw attention or stand out in any way. The second reason had been for the saloon's ample boot space.

He had purchased a pair of powerful binoculars and now used them to scan the houses, eventually picking out Preet Du Plessis' property, checking it against the satellite image printout that Stewart had given him back in London. Many houses in South Africa were equipped with extensive security features designed to deter intruders and safeguard residents. Strands of razor wire were commonly installed along the tops of boundary walls, providing a formidable barrier against trespassers. In addition to razor wire, robust iron fencing and heavy gates offered further layers of protection, making it difficult for anyone to access properties without permission.

Surveillance technology was another prevalent aspect of home security. Closed-circuit television systems monitored entrances and perimeters, recording any suspicious activity. This property was no exception, reflecting the widespread concerns about safety among homeowners in the region. King had already observed private security vehicles patrolling the neighbourhood, a routine sight in many suburbs. These companies often provided 'armed response officers' ready to intervene in emergencies, as well as 'patrol dogs' trained to detect and deter threats. While South African gun ownership did not reach the levels seen in America, it was nevertheless common for residents to keep a firearm at home for self-defence, underscoring the general sense of caution that prevailed throughout the community.

King had spent considerable time poring over the official files on Preet Du Plessis, compiled by both the South African police and Interpol. His research led him to suspect that Du Plessis was protected by a steady flow of bribes, which seemed to keep the South African authorities from pursuing him too closely. The evidence suggested that Du Plessis' ability to evade justice within South Africa was not so much due to a lack of incriminating information, but rather the effectiveness of his corrupt dealings.

Through his investigation, King discovered that Interpol's powers were, in reality, quite limited. The international agency relied heavily on the cooperation and will of local law enforcement in the country concerned. Even if Interpol had sufficient grounds to pursue Du Plessis, their efforts would be futile without the active participation of the South African police. In the absence of such support, their only hope would be to wait until Du Plessis travelled abroad, where they might find a more cooperative partnership with local authorities willing to act on Interpol's requests.

King decided that the man would be armed. He could also assume that someone who had led Du Plessis' life would know how to handle himself, and how to expertly handle a weapon. The man had taken Collins off the street, and it was likely that Collins had learned a great deal from the man, and he would not make the mistake of underestimating Collins' ability. Like King, Peter Stewart had honed what was already there. The tough Scotsman had not started from scratch with either man. The last thing he could afford to do now was underestimate Preet Du Plessis.

King opened the case resting beside him on the

passenger seat. The gun was in pieces, and although he had never used one like it before, he could see that the three sections bolted in place using the hex-key provided. The rifle was fitted with standard V and pin sights, which he would have to assume were set up for fifty to one hundred metres, which was standard. He would like to have practised with it first, but it wasn't possible. He would simply have to wing it.

King assembled the weapon, then unscrewed the plate in the bottom of the pistol-style grip and inserted the 12g $CO_2$ gas cannister and screwed the plate back in, which hissed briefly as the cannister was punctured. Next, he took one of the darts and studied it before taking the sleeping drug and checking the chart in the booklet. He had stolen the tranquiliser gun from a veterinary practice in the nearby town of Paarl. King studied the chart and figured that Preet Du Plessis was larger than a wild dog and smaller than a Springbok, but he had never been on a safari tour, so he flicked on through the pages and thought that the man was a whole lot smaller than a dairy cow. Maybe the man was the size of a leopard? He thought this for no other reason than a leopard was pictured next. King knew that they could leap ten feet into a tree with an antelope in its mouth, so they had to be quite sizeable to do that. He took the jar labelled as *tiletamine-zolazepam* and inserted the needle through the corked neck, then noticed that the booklet stated 2mg per kilo of bodyweight. That made it far easier, and he estimated the man to be around 80kg. He pulled the tranquiliser through the syringe and hesitated as it levelled on 160mg, then kept pulling for a few more for luck. He then studied the dart before unscrewing the tip and filling the reservoir. When he reassembled the dart, he filled another but that used up his entire supply of the tranquiliser, and he just had to hope that he hit his target with at least one of his two shots.

King watched the house through the binoculars again, knowing that he would simply have to settle into the dull routine of surveillance. He had with him plenty of water, a flask of strong, sweet tea that he had brewed back in his hotel room, and a bag of mixed nuts with dried fruit, as well as a bag of biltong – the South African dried meat with its distinct spices. King had learned early in his career to avoid carbohydrates. He had once stuffed his face with fish and chips during a long watch in the rain on a harbour quay and had struggled to stay awake throughout the afternoon shift.

Du Plessis came out of his house and walked to his car three hours later. King almost missed it, but he watched the man back the car out of his driveway, the electric gates opening seamlessly as he reversed into the road. King would have done it differently. He never parked nose-first because he knew the importance of a quick getaway. He would also have checked outside the gates first, because he wouldn't chance driving into an ambush. South Africa was a dangerous place, and you were never more vulnerable than getting in or out of your vehicle. The fact that he had witnessed this 'rookie mistake' boosted his confidence. However, King still had no idea how long the tranquiliser dart would take to incapacitate the man, and he did not want to get into a shootout on the street, because right now, Preet Du Plessis was his only link to Richard Collins.

The South African's house was the last resort in King's assessment. The area was affluent and the entire neighbourhood had CCTV, and he did not want his actions caught on camera. He had also decided that he would be hemmed in. If it all went wrong – and he had concluded that it generally did – then he would be in a firefight in a courtyard of concrete walls and ricochets could ruin everyone's day. Instead, King turned the car around in the road, parked in the adjacent layby that offered panoramic views of the bay, and simply waited.

When he caught sight of Du Plessis's Range Rover in his rearview mirror, he started the engine and held the vehicle on its biting point. As the Range Rover beared down on him, he indicated and pulled out into the road, continuing far enough over the white line for Du Plessis to have no chance in swerving around the collision. As metal scraped against metal, King instantly flicked on the hazard lights and stopped on the side of the road. When he got out, he held his head in both hands and started shouting, "No! No! No!" He looked in the man's direction and shouted, "Oh my God! I'm so sorry!" He studied the damage to the Toyota, quite unthreateningly and walked towards the Range Rover. "It's all my fault! Your beautiful car, I'm so sorry..." King knew that it was the brand-new redesign, a world away from the old P38A as it was known in the trade. This vehicle had upped Land Rover's game. A Rolls Royce for off-road. Naturally, Preet Du Plessis was scathing. "My insurance will take care of it all," King added amiably. "I paid for the best insurance option at Hertz..."

"You fucking moron!" Du Plessis said as he got out of the vehicle. King could see the shape of an automatic underneath the man's sweater.

"I get it. You're upset," said King. "I'm sorry, but my insurance will handle it. I'll get the details so you can be on your way. It's only bodywork..."

Du Plessis walked around the bonnet to assess the damage and broke into a tirade of expletives. He was midway through shouting after King and turning towards him when the dart thudded into his ribcage. King didn't bother with a follow-up shot because it would have stopped the man's heart, so he tossed the tranquiliser gun over the edge of the cliff and ducked down behind the Toyota as the man staggered into the road, pulling his gun and trying to aim it at King. He dropped to his knees, his aim all over the place, then two gunshots passed harmlessly over King's head as the man collapsed.

King moved quickly. He ran to Du Plessis, pocketed the man's Beretta and dragged him to the back of his car. Looking around briefly to check that he was in the clear, he popped open the boot and heaved the South African inside before checking him for more weapons. King smiled as he removed a tactical lock knife and a tiny 'Baby' Browning .25 from an ankle holster. *The cunning bastard,* he thought, knowing it could certainly have ruined his day. King bound the man's hands behind his back using two sets of heavy-duty cable ties and closed the boot lid as a vehicle trundled past without stopping. In South Africa, people did not go out of their way to get into trouble and tended to mind their own business.

## Chapter Forty-Two
### Hout Bay Harbour

King had driven the coast road to the harbour, where he had bought a small day fishing boat three days before. The twenty-eight-foot fast fisher was equipped with twin 300hp Suzuki outboards, GPS, ship-to-shore radio and he had made sure that its four fuel tanks were full.

Getting Preet Du Plessis to the boat proved challenging. Once the man had regained consciousness, King opted for walking him straight to the boat keeping his hands secured with the cable ties, and a knife digging into his ribs just enough to break the skin and remind him how it would go if he decided to resist. Once aboard, King pushed the man down into the basic cuddy cabin, which was little more than a storage area with bench seating with a large crescent-shaped sea cushion on each side. Life jackets, oars, coils of rope, a spare anchor and life rings gave Du Plessis little room but to sit in the middle where the two bench seats met in the prow. King left the door pinned back so he could observe the South African while he stood behind the wheel and started the engines. He cast off the ropes stern and aft and motored out into the lane between two buoys until he cleared the swinging moorings, then piled on the throttles and headed directly out to sea.

King had thought long and hard about how to interrogate his prisoner. He had needed a place to do it, and he had needed somewhere where noise would not be an issue. He had also given great thought on the twelve-hour flight to Cape Town on how he imagined Preet Du Plessis would act with a gun in his face. The man had been around guns and death and violence his entire life. He may well call King's bluff, he may well accept that he was a dead man and wait for a swift release. There had to be something more than the threat of death, or the science of waterboarding that would loosen the man's lips. Slowly, a plan came to King. Nature was a hell of a thing. Beautiful, dangerous, and utterly out of man's control. It was brutal, and it was random. *And that,* thought King, *was part of the terror.*

King knew that at his height of a shade under six foot and perched three feet above the water he could expect to lose sight of land at around six miles out. However, the coast was peppered with mountains, many with flat summits like Cape Town's famous landmark Table Mountain, so he could still see land when the GPS was indicating that he was nine miles offshore. There were no other vessels in the vicinity, other than ocean going tankers at least three miles further towards the horizon. King killed the engines and ducked inside the cabin, pulling Du Plessis to his feet and out through the hatch. He marched the man without ceremony to the stern and cut the cable ties. Du Plessis rubbed his wrists, the plastic having cut deeply into his flesh, but he hadn't expected to be shoved over the transom and into the icy water. When he surfaced, he was spluttering and cursing and kicking wildly. King pushed him away from the boat using a fishing gaff. The metal hook was honed to a razor-sharp tip, but Du Plessis tried to grab it, merely slicing his hands in the process and leaving clouds of blood in the water as he sculled to stay afloat.

"I'm going to ask you some questions," said King. "And you're going to answer them..."

"Fuck you!"

King shrugged and headed to the wheel where he started the engines and hit the throttles, surging the boat forwards before pulling back on the twin throttles. The boat was still moving, drifting forty feet from the South African. "Where is Collins?"

"I said... fuck you!"

King nodded and picked up one of four buckets fitted with lids that were strapped to the transom. He peeled off the plastic lid and threw the contents towards Du Plessis. The man frowned, then screamed when he saw the fish heads, fish skins, guts and blood drifting towards him in a thick, wide slick. The bucket had a twenty-litre capacity, which equated to a hell of a lot of fish waste.

"You can pay a fortune for a great white shark experience in South Africa," said King. "But I guess it's quite different in a cage. A lot safer, I'd imagine..." He paused, watching the man splashing in the water. King was an expert swimmer, and he could tell by the way that the man treaded water that he was not comfortable out of his depth, let alone nine miles out where the Atlantic and Indian oceans met. He imagined that a few lengths of a pool and swim up to the pool bar was more the man's scene. "You and Collins brought down the airliner with the Rwandan president onboard," said King. "Collins worked for us. We want Collins. It's as simple as that. Tell me where he is, and I'll take you back to shore."

## Crossfire

"You won't. I know how it works," he spluttered.

King nodded with grim determination and reached for another bucket, his actions deliberate and methodical. He removed the plastic lid, exposing the foul contents within. Without hesitation, King tossed the bucket's contents towards Du Plessis, the mass of fish waste spreading out across the water, the fish oils glimmering in the sun. Du Plessis coughed and spluttered, his eyes fixed on the slick, intensifying his discomfort and fear. As Du Plessis struggled, desperate to swim back towards the boat, King maintained his composure and quickly returned to the helm. He hit the throttles, ensuring he kept a safe distance between the vessel and the panicked man in the water. Once again, King set the boat in neutral, allowing it to drift quietly with the four-stroke engines idling almost silently, their low hum barely audible above the lapping of the swell on the boat's hull.

"Tell me, and I'll take you back to shore."

"I'm not stupid... you can't take the chance of me telling Richard that I talked..."

King nodded. Stewart had made it clear that Preet Du Plessis didn't get a way out of this. He sparked a war that had cost a million lives to date. Collins had tipped off the Ugandans and Stewart's team had been killed. Not only that, but because of Collins' treachery, Britain had lost its hope for trade deals, and precious resources and minerals contracts. The last thing the higher echelons of MI6 and the UK government were going to allow was Collins and Du Plessis plying their trade without recourse.

King looked past the man, struggling to stay afloat, cupping his hand over his eyes as he watched the water against the glare of the sun. "That's the first fin," he lied, watching as Du Plessis spun around in the water spluttering and kicking wildly. "I thought a great white would ambush from the deep. But it looks like you're getting some advanced warning..."

"Get me out!" the man screamed, spinning back around and stroking for the boat.

King tossed in another bucket of guts and hit the throttles for a couple of seconds. When he knocked the throttles back into neutral and started to drift, Du Plessis was fifty metres from him, stroking wildly through the water. King wasn't a sadist but didn't exactly feel sorry for the man. Three hundred and thirty souls onboard the plane, a million more on the ground. But it wasn't just that. Collins had bid his farewell by killing Ginnie and trying to frame King. He had sparked a war, but what had happened to Lucinda was down to Collins and Du Plessis's roll of the dice. Stewart had been adamant that the man should get what was coming to him, and King was not only in full agreement, but was happy to do what needed to be done. But he *had* to make the man talk first.

"Do you think a large great white would sever your leg cleanly, or drag you down to the depths?" King asked as the man drew near. "Have you seen the film *Jaws*? Of course you have, everybody has. That blonde girl got pulled around a bit at the beginning of the film, didn't she? I always thought that looked realistic. Coughing, spluttering, begging..." He shivered at the thought.

"Fuck you!" Du Plessis screamed. "Get me out of here!"

"The water is cold," King continued. "Do you think that will make a difference to the pain? I mean, if you hit your thumb with a hammer on a cold day, it hurts like hell..." He touched the throttles and left him in his wake. This time, he motored on and turned a wide arc, leaving the man a few hundred metres behind him. He slowly completed the

## Crossfire

circle, watching Du Plessis give up on swimming and tread water. The man's head was spinning around him like an owl as he desperately searched for a shark fin, for all the good spotting one would do him.

King thought about Ginnie. Naked, dying in fear and a state of humiliation, all dignity lost. He thought about Lucinda and her ordeal, what she would have to live with. He did not know her cameraman or editor, but he felt their barbaric penalty for reporting the truth a personal blow by association. He slowed as he neared Du Plessis, and picked up the last bucket, peeling off the lid and tossing the entire bucket into the ocean, where it bobbed semi-submerged, mixing slowly with the water, the blood and animal waste pulsing into the sea with every rise and fall of the swells.

"I'm getting bored of this, Du Plessis..." King said as he watched the man tire from treading water. "You know where Richard Collins is. Let's not kid each other any further. You can drown, which is a horrible death. Or you can get torn to shreds when a shark comes for the blood. Did you know that they can sense a thimbleful of blood in a million parts water? There's now eighty litres of the stuff in there with you, in the capital of great white territory..." He paused, pulling the man's own 9mm Beretta from his waistband. "Or you can have a bullet in the head. Lights out, no drama..."

Du Plessis stared at King, finally understanding that fate had caught up with him. When you live by the sword, you can expect to die by the sword. King could see the look of resignation in the man's eyes, but more than that; he realised that if he stayed in the game long enough then he too could expect both his luck and time to run out. What fate would await King if he continued down this path?

King's thoughts were cut short when he saw a shadow

in the water. He supposed this could always have been a possibility, but in truth he had not thought that far ahead. He had merely wanted to terrify the truth out of Preet Du Plessis, but now the action had consequences. Du Plessis saw the look of recognition in King's eyes and panicked even more, shouting, thrashing and kicking and doing just about everything the textbooks told you not to do.

"Please!"

"Where is he?"

"Greece!"

"Where?"

Preet Du Plessis choked on a mouthful of seawater and gagged, struggling to speak, but aware that he had to if he was going to avoid being attacked. King seriously doubted that the man would expect a ride back to shore, and the thought that the man was desperate for a quick death was not lost on him. He was left conflicted at the thought of the power he had over him, supreme, even God-like.

The shark broke the water, gliding between Du Plessis and the boat. King estimated the creature to be fourteen feet in length, and with the girth of a pony. Its movements were imperceptible, and yet it cruised faster than King could ever hope to swim, the merest sway of its tailfin propelling it through the water, and then it was gone. Millions of years of apex predation, not evolving since before dinosaurs walked the earth. The grey of its back barely visible a metre under the surface, its white belly invisible to creatures below it as it used sunlight and shadows to keep it invisible. King had seen enough nature documentaries to know that when the great white attacked, its prey never saw it coming, and the speed it could generate in a short, frenzied energy, would be like being hit by a car. With three hundred razor-sharp teeth. The sight of the creature was almost overwhelming, such was its size and cold, deadly beauty.

King raised the pistol, and Du Plessis saw his chance, his escape from one of the worst deaths imaginable. "A small island near Milos! That's all I know! It's tiny, just fishing boats and a small village. No tourism…"

King aimed the pistol and Du Plessis closed his eyes. The sights centred on the man's forehead, and in that moment, King thought about Ginnie again, of Lucinda. The chain of events that had led to more than a million deaths in Rwanda. He lowered the pistol, then tossed it into the ocean and settled in behind the wheel, perching on the seat as he throttled forward and headed towards land. The man did not deserve a swift end. He had caused misery for countless people during his life, his career plying his death trade over the continent. After a few hundred metres, King turned and looked behind him, but Preet Du Plessis was no longer there.

# Chapter Forty-Three
## The Cyclades Islands, Greece

The sun shimmered on the mirrored surface of the Aegean Sea and even wearing the pair of Ray-Ban sunglasses that he had purchased just hours before in the duty free at Gatwick, King found himself squinting at the intensity of the light. There was something about the light in the Greek Islands, the purity of it that made it utterly unique. The sun occupied a cloudless sky, searing and relentless and it was difficult to see where the ocean met the sky on an ambiguous horizon. Cicadas electrified the wispy pines and poplars, and tiny lizards scurried from King's boots as he climbed the natural steps in the cliff path worn over millennia by erosion and footsteps alike. This was harsh territory that had been tamed by stubborn mankind. Below King, the horseshoe cove was the beginning and the end for weary fishermen. Small boats had been launched and hauled back over the pebbles for thousands of years, the only difference now being the smoky, oily outboard engines and the nylon nets hanging for repair from the cliffs. The houses and fishing huts had probably changed little, too. Now painted a brilliant white which reflected the punishing sun, with a few of the buildings fitted with satellite dishes and air-conditioning units. This was a quiet island with little tourism but for a few cheap Airbnb properties on the northern side and a campsite popular with gap-year students and New Age hippies alike. King could see reason in Collins choosing this island. No crowds, no regular police presence – the island fell under the jurisdiction of the larger island of Milos – and the man would be able to secure his base, guard himself from attack. However, the remote, anonymous location could also be the man's undoing. King had found him easily because the locals all knew about the stranger living on their island, who ran the cliffs and swam in the bays to keep fit, who bought freshly landed fish from the cove and who queued for bread and vegetables at the island's daily market. They knew that he had purchased the tiny fisherman's cottage, or *syrmata*, nestled into the cliff on the east side of the island. When the ninety-year-old fisherman had died in his sleep, his family – now living on the mainland – had put the property up for auction and, a few weeks later, the man they called 'The Hermit' had arrived and other than a few fishermen and the woman on the vegetable stall and the old baker, and the family who ran the island's only convenience store had spoken to nobody else in two months. In a small island community, this was both noticeable and controversial.

King had always known that the best place to hide was in a crowd, and as he drew closer to the next cove – where he had been reliably informed was where 'The Hermit's' house was hewn into the cliffs – his suspicions were confirmed. Collins was sitting on a roughly finished concrete terrace just a few feet above the calm sea, a cotton sheet spread out like a sail above his head to afford him some shade. He was reading a paperback and beside him a bottle of some sort of clear spirit and a glass. King watched him for longer than he should have, wondering whether this was the fate of assassins who had been hung out to dry. The life of a hermit until they sent a man to kill you. Either way, it didn't look good, and he knew that he needed a better retirement plan than Collins.

King did not check the CZ75 pistol that was tucked into his belt. He had loaded the 9mm pistol and made it ready earlier on the island of Crete where it had been waiting for him buried in the gravelly sand like pirate treasure. A text message with detailed instructions had led him to the weapon, and it had been wrapped in an oiled cloth and sealed inside a plastic freezer bag. King estimated the distance to Collins and his rough elevation. He figured on a hundred metres with fifty metres of drop. Could he put some rounds on the target with those figures? Certainly. On paper, at least. But at a human target, it was another matter entirely. Not worth the risk. Especially when the target was a highly trained assassin. Still, there was no other alternative. The sea was so clear, so crystalline that King could not hope to swim up to Collins, and the man had a full view of the cliff. A rifle would have made all the difference, but he was working on the fly, and he couldn't have carried even a disassembled rifle to the island on the tiny water taxi. He checked the opposite cliff, then looked back at Collins, but the man was no longer there. King felt a flutter in his stomach and a surge of adrenaline. If Collins had gone inside the tiny house, then he had a chance to descend the cliff and get closer. He dropped his day sack on the rocks and started down the cliff path. It would have been easy for a mountain goat, but a lot trickier for King, who settled on leaping down every few steps, his desert boots taking the impact out of the soles of his feet. The steps had been cut from flat rocks and worn smooth over time. Islanders would have traversed the path for hundreds if not thousands of years, but likely not as rapidly as King as he rushed to get out of Collins' line of sight when he returned to his shady seat and half-finished bottle.

King drew the pistol when he was on the last few steps and dropped into the shade. There were no windows on the cliff side of the *syrmata*. A fisherman only cared about the sea. King caught his breath in the shade; his weapon trained on the side of the building. Edging nearer, he kept checking the other side anxious that he had nobody to cover his rear. There was a time when Collins would have taken care of that, and the two men had worked together as a formidable team.

Collins was back in his deckchair, the makeshift sail billowing above his head. He had the glass in his left hand, and the bottle was on the ground casting a long shadow towards King.

"I was wondering who they would send," said Collins.

"And I always knew..." King commented flatly as he walked around the concrete terrace and put the sun behind his back, forcing Collins to squint into the sun.

"I was always better than you."

"And yet I'm the one with a gun in my hand..."

Collins raised his glass slowly. "To the delicious taste of death..." he said, then took a sip. "And to the assassin's aim... steady and true..."

"Steady and true..." King said quietly, his grip tightening on the pistol as he minutely adjusted his aim.

"And one last drink?" Collins smiled and brought the glass to his lips. "One for the road, so to speak..."

King allowed his former colleague and comrade the courtesy and watched as the man knocked back the drink, but before he had drained the glass, he dropped it clumsily and it fell to the ground, catching the light before it smashed on the concrete plinth. Smoke and mirrors. Balls and cups. The sleight of hand had taken King's concentration – only momentarily, but it had been enough. Collins had the tiny automatic in his hand and King knew as he adjusted his aim that the man had set his own sights on him fractionally quicker. He saw the muzzle flash, heard the gunshot and felt the bite of the bullet as he squeezed the trigger. Two more gunshots and King staggered backwards, losing his footing and falling into the water.

King's reaction was to swim away, but he could not risk turning his back on his enemy. He was suspended in the water looking upwards, the surface three feet above him. He could see the man step up to the edge of the rocks. Blood wafted in front of him, but he still held the pistol and brought it to bear. He fired twice, watching as Collins staggered backwards. He doubted that the bullets had reached him, three feet was about the limit of a bullet fired in water, but King broke the surface and followed up with two more shots as he sculled backwards with his feet and free hand. The pain was searing on his torso, but he grit his teeth and fired another three shots, watching as Collins ducked and returned fire, but he had bought himself time and was already on the cusp of the tiny automatic's range. Another dozen strokes and he was around the rocky outcrop and in the shelter of the headland.

King was fading fast. He dropped the pistol and rolled onto his front, forcing his battered body to crawl around the headland. Every movement grew more laboured, his limbs sluggish and heavy. He could feel himself sagging, the sharp pain in his side threatening to tip him into unconsciousness.

**Crossfire**

The saltwater stung his eyes, blurring his vision further, while the world around him seemed to tilt and darken.

The water became deeper here, the reassuring firmness of the ocean floor slipping away beneath him, leaving only darkness below. King struggled to keep moving, but his arms no longer obeyed him. He became aware that they were floating limply in front of him, useless and weightless. As he drifted, the seabed loomed closer, the light above growing ever fainter. The oppressive silence was broken only by the ache in his ears, the pressure of the water increasing as he descended helplessly towards the blackness, his consciousness ebbing away.

## Chapter Forty-Four
### Milos, Greece

King was gripped by an overwhelming thirst, an intensity he had never known before. As he struggled onward, waves of confusion washed over him, repeatedly dragging his mind between fleeting moments of awareness and the looming void of unconsciousness. Each time he surfaced from the darkness, clarity slipped away again, leaving him suspended on the edge of oblivion, his senses battered by the relentless cycle of fading and returning consciousness. He was aware of somebody beside him and felt firm, yet comforting hands on his wrist and caught the unmistakable scent of a woman, felt her body press into him, yet there was nothing sexual about it. Still, he could not open his eyes, but he felt the woman's warm breath as she spoke to him in a language he did not understand.

"It is okay..." she said in heavily accented English. "You are well, and waking up *unquickly*... I mean, slowly..." King tried to respond but his words stuck in his throat. He felt a cool, wet flannel on his lips and found himself sucking water through the material, his mouth slowly loosening. He squinted through the darkness, the bright sunlight reflecting through the window and off the whitewashed walls. The flannel was replaced with a paper cup, and he felt the water bring his dried and crusted lips back to life. "Slowly!" she said. "Just sip *sippy* sip..."

King ignored her instructions and drank greedily, desperate to quench the unbearable thirst that had plagued him since regaining consciousness. He felt the cup being gently taken from his grasp, and, as he looked up towards the source of the voice, his vision finally began to clear. The woman before him was unremarkable in appearance, her features plain and without any hint of conventional beauty. Yet, in that moment, she was the most welcome presence he could have imagined. To King, she was a vision of hope and salvation, and he regarded her with the profound gratitude of someone who had been granted a second chance at life.

"Right nurse, you can leave us to it now..." Stewart's gruff Scottish tone echoed off the stone walls and finally brought King round from his transitioning state.

The nurse looked over King and shrugged. "Ten minutes, no more, he needs..."

"*Sleepy* sleep *sleepy*?" Stewart asked mockingly. "Don't worry, he's a big boy. You can give him a bed bath later..."

King attempted to push himself up the bed, but he gasped in pain and dropped onto his back. He could not see Stewart from where he was sitting on the other side of the room, but the man slowly came into view as he limped to the bed, his face creased in a scowl.

"What the fuck was that?"

"I appear to be alive," King replied. "Thanks for asking."

"You allowed him to get the better of you."

"It happens, I suppose."

"Yes, it does. But it generally happens to dead people."

"Did I get him?"

Stewart smirked. "No King, you did not..."

"Oh..."

"You're one lucky bastard, though."

"Really?" King licked his already parched lips, and Stewart picked up the cup and held it for him to sip from. It was a rare gesture of kindness that caught King off guard. When he had slaked his thirst, King said, "It really doesn't feel like I'm very lucky."

"You are. You took three bullets. It's a good job Collins used a twenty-five." Stewart shrugged, shaking his head. "He seems to have forgotten everything I taught him, too. Never fuck about with anything less than a thirty-eight..."

"Well, I'm glad he did," said King pointedly. Stewart sighed and dragged a chair beside the bed. "What happened to me?" he asked. "I mean, after I got shot, that is."

Stewart shrugged. "A fisherman and his son were just around the headland from you when they heard the gunshots. They were harvesting scallops. The son was in the water diving down to get them, and the father was packing them away in boxes of ice onboard the boat. The lad dived down and pulled you to the surface and they headed for Milos. A coastguard vessel picked you up and took you the rest of the way after they radioed for help."

"Shit..." King mused. "I really *was* lucky..."

"Luck is a commodity that is quickly depleted." Stewart paused. "The only way we can control luck is to prepare. If you took a damned rifle to the island, then Collins would be brown bread, and you'd be sipping a beer on a beach and checking out the talent." He shrugged. "And if Collins hadn't chosen a gun more suited to a lady's handbag to protect himself with, then it could well have been a different story for him, too."

## Crossfire

King nodded. He'd always known that the best lessons in life were the most painful ones, but he wasn't about to start feeling good about it. "So, he's in the wind..." he stated flatly.

"The wind blows, but it must stop sometime. When it does, we'll catch up with him." Stewart paused. "What about Preet Du Plessis?"

"He won't be starting another war, that's for sure."

"Any chance of comebacks?"

"None," King replied firmly.

"That's all I need to know." He stood up, reached into his pocket and retrieved an envelope, which he tossed onto the bed beside King. "There's fifteen grand in there. Stay in the islands, get better and get yourself a tan. Come back when you're well enough to work, or when the money runs out. Don't worry about the local cops, it's all been cleared."

King watched the man walk out of the room without looking back. He picked up the envelope and reached painfully to put it in the bedside cupboard. As he closed the door, the nurse came back inside and topped up his paper cup of water from a jug.

"You must drink, but slowly and not too much," she told him. King sipped the water, his equilibrium finally returning. He tried moving again and winced at the pain and the nurse reached up and adjusted the feed of painkiller next to the antibiotic bag on the drip. King felt at ease almost at once. "This is opioid based, so you will feel maybe a little drunk," she explained. "But you will be out of bed tomorrow. The doctor will see you on his rounds this afternoon."

King nodded. "What time is it?"

The nurse opened the cupboard and rummaged around, handing King his watch. "Eleven. You came out of surgery an hour ago and was in there for twelve hours. I don't know how long it took to get you to Milos, but you are a very lucky man..."

"So, they keep saying..." King replied sardonically.

"Your friend will come back and see you?" she asked. "He is very rude man!"

"Oh, yeah, he's rude alright," King replied. "But he's not my friend..." The nurse smiled awkwardly and King watched her leave, not knowing what was worse: the fact that he was lying in bed with multiple gunshot wounds, or that Stewart was in fact, the only friend he had in the world.

## Chapter Forty-Five
### Six weeks later, Cornwall

King rested the axe head on the ground, fully aware that he had already pushed himself too far. Despite the ache in his body, he surveyed the neat pile of split logs, satisfied that he now had enough to keep the fire going. With a final effort, he drove the axe deep into the chopping block, marking the end of his work for the day, and turned towards the house, heading inside. There was a strange feeling that lingered with him; manual labour was something entirely new to him. King had never engaged in this kind of physical work before, and he realised now that he had underestimated the time it would take for his wounds to heal. The cluster of scars on his body would be a permanent reminder of Richard Collins, a part of him that could never be erased.

Inside the cottage the story was much the same as the gardens, and he felt somewhat overwhelmed that he did not know where to start. He supposed a good clean would be the way to go, and then he would dab some plaster and slap some paint on the walls. How hard could it be? Surely plastering would be like buttering toast, but on a larger scale?

He had found the wooden floors more difficult than he had first anticipated, so he supposed plastering would be just as hard. He had sanded and stained the floors and now wondered if he should have left that job to last after painting. Paint could drip and ruin his work on the floor. This was going to be a hell of a learning curve. But not the last.

"What a fucking dump..."

King cursed as he turned to Stewart. He had let down his guard. A month of sunning himself on the beaches of the Greek islands had slowed him down and although he had healed and rested well, he could feel his alertness and fitness waning. "Tea?"

"Of course."

King led the way into the small kitchen and put the kettle on the Aga. He had learnt that the Aga could take anywhere between a few minutes and half a day to boil the kettle, depending on how organised he was with the wood and which way the wind was blowing.

"When did you get this place?"

"The sale completed while I was recuperating in Greece."

"I suppose it'll be nice when it's finished..."

King shrugged. "Yeah, that's obviously the plan," King replied sardonically.

"But, why the hell in Cornwall of all places?"

King took two mugs out of the cupboard and tested the side of the kettle with his fingertips. It was looking promising. The fire was still in, and a draught was finding its way to the bottom of the stove. "It's my bolthole. Beaches, cliff walks, woodland, nice pubs..."

"Storms, rain, damp air... bleak, grey and deserted in the winter... busy roads and beaches all summer..." Stewart scoffed. "It's isolated, though. I'll certainly give you that."

## Crossfire

King made the tea. It was over a four-hour drive to London, and it took just as long on the train. This is what King liked about the location the most. He still had the flat in Wandsworth, provided to him by the service. Stewart liked to have his agents close, which was why he was finding issues with King's bolthole. But King realised that he needed space. Cornwall was the answer to this. It wasn't on the way to anywhere.

"When can we expect you back?" Stewart said, taking the mug of tea from him and taking a sip. He placed the mug back down on the kitchen table, reached into his inside jacket pocket for his silver hip flask and proceeded to add a generous measure of Scotch. Twenty-year old MacCallan was King's bet. Stewart did not live an extravagant life; he drove a ten-year-old Jaguar and lived with his wife, Margaret in a bungalow on the edge of a suburban estate near a canal, but King had seen the man drop seven hundred pounds on a bottle of whisky without even blinking.

"Can you give me a week, boss?"

Stewart nodded. "It'll take more than a week to get this place watertight..."

"Unless it's Collins," said King. "I might be able to find some time if you know where he is..."

"Fancy another go at him already?"

"Of course."

"Not lost your nerve?"

"With respect, boss... fuck off..."

Stewart grinned. "You're the better agent, King. I made a mistake with Collins, others told me, but I didn't listen." He paused. "But hopefully, you learned a valuable lesson that day."

"When you need a pistol, bring a rifle?" King shrugged

and sipped some of his tea. "I wanted to look the bastard in the eye as I squeezed the trigger. For Ginnie..." He didn't add for Lucinda and her crew, or the million poor souls caught in a war of ethnic cleansing because of his actions. He had not told Stewart about Lucinda's rape because Stewart hated the press, hated the fact that King had grown close to a journalist on the Angola job, and hated the woman because of her government connections through her marriage. He wasn't a man to be sensitive, and King was in no mood to get antagonised by his gruff demeanour. He had simply asked for some intel on Colonel Jones and had not told the man what he had intended to do with it.

"Never does anyone any good," Stewart replied. "So, you tell them whatever it is you want them to hear in their final moments, and then you switch off their lights. They no longer know anything, let alone give a shit. It's a fool's errand. The job is the job, and personal crap will always get in the way. Trust me, I've done the dramatic death thing to pay back fallen comrades, and it's a waste of time." He paused. "Bullet to the back of the head, job done."

"I'll bear that in mind, when I find him."

"Collins will keep. He's gone to ground, and I taught him how to stay there. When he breaks cover, we'll kill him. Plain and simple," Stewart said pointedly. "I have something else for you. Something that will ease you back into it."

"Right..."

"You remember Jane Hargreaves?"

King did. She was an analyst with MI6 and had been part of a contingent assessing Britain's oil trade agreements and tenders in Angola. Taken hostage along with a government minister and OPEC executives, Jane had later escaped and helped King rescue the hostages. When they had returned to England they had gone on a couple of dates together, but it hadn't stuck. Work, mainly. Opportunities missed.

"She's left SIS and joined the flat foots over at Five. She's working with the new Middle East desk run by Charles Forrester. He's a bit of a geek, but a solid bloke. I gather he's in line for the deputy director's job when he leaves. They're heading out to Beirut and well, since you and Collins royally fucked up that job, you can be their bodyguard and tidy a few loose ends at the same time."

"Bodyguard?"

"Yeah, it's easy. You work out how someone would likely kill the people you're protecting, then see that they don't. Nobody is better placed to keep someone alive, than somebody who had been trained to kill."

"Just don't get involved," said Stewart. "Jane is attractive, intelligent and easy to talk to."

King shrugged. "What makes you think I'd get involved?"

"Because you do. Lucinda Davenport? Ginnie Blake?" Stewart chided. "Your job is to shadow her. Shadows stay at the front, or the side, or behind... they are never on top..."

King said nothing. But he thought about Jane. He liked her, and he liked the idea of working with her. For the first time in over a month he felt a renewed vigour towards his work. The job sounded like a challenge. Exciting, and not just for the opportunity to work with Jane. He knew how it would go. Stewart would have a job for him in Beirut and that would provide him with its own set of challenges, but it was a chance to make good on something that had gnawed at him ever since. And how often did a person get the chance to truly redeem themselves in life?

# Author's Note

The next King thriller is: Shockwave

Hi, thanks for reading, and I hope you enjoyed my story!

I'm hard at work writing a new thriller and can't wait to entertain you again soon. I appreciate that you've done your part by purchasing and reading, but if you have time to head over to Amazon to leave a review, or simply rate this, then you would make this author extremely happy!
### *A P Bateman*

To learn more about my books check out www.apbateman.com

Printed in Dunstable, United Kingdom